Blindsided

BLINDSIDED

Chelsea Catherine

TEXAS REVIEW PRESS · HUNTSVILLE, TEXAS

First Edition
Requests for permission to acknowledge material from this work should be sent to:
  Permissions
  Texas Review Press
  English Department
  Sam Houston State University
  Huntsville, TX 77341-2146

Library of Congress Cataloging-in-Publication Data

Names: Catherine, Chelsea, 1990– author.
Title: Blindsided / by Chelsea Catherine.
Description: Huntsville, Texas : Texas Review Press, [2018] |
Identifiers: LCCN 2018008598 (print) | LCCN 2018010958 (ebook) |
  ISBN 9781680031645 (ebook) | ISBN 9781680031638 (pbk.)
Subjects: | LCGFT: Lesbian erotic fiction.
Classification: LCC PS3603.A8973 (ebook) | LCC PS3603.A8973 B55 2018 (print) |
  DDC 813/.6—dc23
LC record available at https://lccn.loc.gov/2018008598

Cover design by Nancy Parsons
Author photo courtesy Liz Megan Rouleau

for the woman who broke my heart;
thanks at least for helping me get published

ONE

The heat this winter is going to drive me crazy. I sit in my office and sweat, even with the air conditioning on full blast. It's too hot for February in Key West. Temperatures have been in the low eighties most days with the humidity around seventy percent. The season sizzles on the streets. People are wound up, ready for something.

My grandmother, Mimi, says it's because something dangerous is coming. I think it's probably just global warming.

Mimi and I are nothing alike. She's ruled by superstition and faith, magic and voodoo. The only thing we have in common is our first name, Eliza, and even then, most people call me Eli. I'm ruled by logic. Algorithms. I run my own business, designing websites and doing freelance marketing and advertising. My office is just north of Key West in a marina on Stock Island. From my desk, I watch fishing boats cruise into the dock, ripples marring the calm water.

I'm finishing up a website for a new customer when the door to my office opens. I turn. My friend, Carla, stands in the doorway. She wears work clothes—grey polyester pants and a white silk top and I can see the rounded tops of her breasts in it, pressed upwards by a good bra. For a woman in her late forties, they look pretty awesome. "What are you doing here?" I ask.

She tucks a piece of black hair behind her ears. Carla is thick. Her skin is white and freckled and her voice is low, slick and oozing like honey from years of smoking. "I wanted to talk."

"And you couldn't call?"

She hesitates, then crosses the room. Her office is downtown, amidst a bunch of new wave health centers and banks. There's no reason for her to come all the way out here unless she wants something. "I'm thinking about running for mayor of Key West," she says, and her eyes immediately go to mine, assessing my reaction.

"Really?"

"I want you to do my marketing and help me with my platform."

"You're a Republican." A smile tugs on the corners of my mouth. "Why should I?"

"Because I'm going to pay you good money." She sits on the edge of the desk, her chest rising and falling unevenly. Nervous. Carla's breath has always conveyed her mood; the first time I met her, I noticed it right away. We sat next to each other at a Business Guild happy hour and spent an extra hour together at the bar after the event finished. I couldn't stop staring at the way her chest moved, how she breathed harder instead of laughing and her smile came out through her eyes. "And because you like me so much."

I smile. "I have a lot going on."

"Come over tomorrow tonight. We can talk about the timeline."

Carla lives on Summerland Key, in a rich neighborhood on the water. I've been friends with her for nine months now, I've spent ten-hour days with her volunteering at Rotary Club events, I know her parents' names. I've tried every dish she's brought to community luncheons, but I've never been invited inside her house. "For real, Carla?"

"I don't care if I win, I just don't want to look like an asshole."

I turn toward the window, rubbing my neck. I feel that flutter I get so often around her, that burn like hot coffee in my chest. She'd be good at politics, in some ways. She's mean. A straight-shooter. People know her here.

Outside, a pelican settles on the side of a small fishing boat. His beak quivers. He sits still for a moment before diving into the silver water. Ripples expand outward. He resurfaces and lands again on the ledge of the boat with a slender snapper. It struggles for several moments in the pelican's beak before being swallowed whole. "Do you think you'll win?" I ask.

"No. I just feel like this will be good for me."

"What's in it for me?"

She gives me a smile and her eyelashes flutter. Then she shifts and the desk creaks under her weight. "Wouldn't you do anything for me?" Her voice is high and nasally, the way it gets when she flirts. Her breasts press at the silk.

"Uh huh," I say.

Her eyes glimmer. "You're the best at this kind of stuff. I trust you."

I stand so we're face to face, just inches away, and I can feel the warmth radiating off her body. Everything about her is fever and false bravado. Predictable. But there's something about the way she looks at me that feels different now.

•••

After Carla leaves, I head home, too. I live ten miles north of Key West on a key called Big Coppitt. Trailers sit dilapidated on the side of dirt roads next to puddles large as kiddie pools. Streetlamps hum with broken electricity. Even the palm trees wilt. The thick air reeks of algae and seagrass.

I rent a studio on the third floor of a large stilt house that's less than 400 square feet but has a full kitchen, semi-walled off bedroom, and private stairwell. From the living room window, I can see the water unobscured. It's not always a pretty place to live, but it's a lot quieter than Key West. Here, there's no party scene, not many snowbirds. No stupid crowds and tourists.

Upstairs, I drop my things on the door hanger and take my shoes off. Wood tiles line the floor. It smells like heat, like sun and dry soil. I have this feeling in my gut, this pressure. It's like I need to take a shit, but I don't. On instinct, I open the kitchen drawer and take out one of the sage sticks Mimi sent me last month.

Sage reminds me of childhood. Mimi is a native Londoner but she moved to the island of Montserrat with my dad in the eighties. That's where I was born and raised. My mom was always gone—drugs and finding trouble. Dad worked a lot so I spent more time with Mimi than with him. She was always playing with crystals, muttering incantations, and sticking things like frankincense under my bed to protect me.

After opening all the windows, I light the sage. The leaves catch quickly and start to burn. I blow on the fire until it smolders, smoke spiraling with the breeze. I start at the base of the wall closest to me and work my way up, gently waving the stick over the walls, mixing the smoke around. The scent, acrid and faintly tart, fills the space.

"I'm clearing this space of negative energy," I tell the room. "I only allow positive energy to be around me."

I repeat this, going from wall to wall until the entire apartment is done. Then I stand in the middle of the living room and wave the stick around myself—starting from my feet and working up to my head.

When I'm done, I place the sage on a plate so it will burn out.

I'm not superstitious. I don't believe in *espiritus* like Mimi does, there's just a feeling I get sometimes. Like I did before the volcano erupted back in Montserrat. I was only seven, but I remember the feeling and shitting my pants for two days before the whole thing went off. Mimi, Dad, and I were at a healer out of town trying to get me stopped up, which is the only reason we got out safely.

Running a hand over the pit of my belly, I open my laptop and start to work. I first look over Carla's Facebook page—nothing terrible strikes me . She's a gun nut, too many pictures of hunting rifles. But then there are the posts about fundraisers and pictures of the work she does with the guild. She's like a parrot, posting and re-posting.

I roll my eyes, make a note of it on a pad of paper, and keep going.

$$\bullet \bullet \bullet$$

I can't stop thinking about Carla the next day and can barely focus at work. I feel like some barrier between us has been broached—she's never invited me over before. Never asked for anything this serious from me. It's late by the time I make my way up to her house. Her neighborhood in Summerland Key is all rich people. Howard Livingston lives here. The Mile Marker 24 Band truck sits out front.

I drive slow, watching the houses grow in size. One has a see-through glass elevator. Another has an outdoor spiral staircase that looks like it's made from white marble. It's so different from my neighborhood, the trailers and tiny stilt homes with chickens scattered about.

Finally, I reach Carla's house. It sits near the end of the drive and hidden partially by a small fence. Night blankets the canal water an inky black. Bougainvillea and sea grape bushes line the front yard. It's immaculately kept—she pays someone to tend to it, like most of the people here. I park outside and climb the stairs to the second floor, then knock. Carla hollers to let myself in.

The inside of her house is completely different from the outside. It looks like her office has exploded all over everything. The floors are clean but pieces of paper lay in stacks in the hallway. Open accordion files litter the kitchen table. It smells like meatloaf.

I feel immensely satisfied. Seeing her house like this, messy, untamed, confirms that part of her can't be in control, that part of her really does go beyond the practiced smiles at Rotary meetings. It feels fundamental to who she is; Carla seesaws between light and dark, exposing herself, then covering. I never tire of watching her shift back and forth. "Carla?"

Footsteps echo from the hallway to my right. Then Carla

emerges. She's barefoot and in jeans, a lavender v-neck that clings to her curves. "Work is busy," she says, nodding to the stacks. "I made meatloaf."

I stare. "Do you have anything to drink?"

She moves around me to enter the kitchen. I've never seen her dressed like this. She seems so unguarded. Normally, I sit across from her at lunch or next to her at a guild or Rotary meeting. Usually she's in pressed pants and silk blouses, the top two buttons undone so only a slight hint of cleavage peeks out. "I only have tequila."

"That'll do."

I place my laptop on the table. The wood is polished but stained. Although I know she has a twenty-year-old son at the University of Florida, I feel like a child has never lived here. The walls are barren, the furniture unkempt, but clean. A single picture of Miles rests on the living room wall—him in his Conch lacrosse uniform, black shaggy hair hanging over his eyes and his thick neck straining against the collar.

Carla takes two glasses out of the cabinet, her ass jiggling as she slides against the countertop. "How do you want it?"

I smile. "On the rocks," I say, before starting up my laptop and pushing away some of her papers. They're real estate agreements, handwritten. Carla's handwriting is beautiful—small but with a rounded flare, especially on her uppercase letters like her P's and R's. It's girly and neat. Soft and unlike her.

A few seconds later, she pads over and places one of the glasses next to me, full with round ice cubes. The other fizzes slightly. From the smell, I think it's tonic water.

I try to focus on work but being this close to her, in her home like this, makes me feel like I'm crawling out of my skin. I reach immediately for the tequila and take a deep gulp. Heat branches across my chest. It's smooth and light.

"What's wrong?" she asks. Her eyes fill with light then crinkle. "Are you worried this is a first date?"

"You wish." On the screen, an old professional picture of her stares back at me from her LinkedIn page. Her hair was shorter. Her skin is smoother and her smile makes her look cherubic, like a different person.

...

For two hours, I pour over her social media. I delete everything damning and clean up her photos while she draws up paperwork for a house in Big Pine. Her cell phone keeps ringing—different buyers, she says. She doesn't answer any of them.

By ten o'clock we've only picked at the meatloaf but have killed a third of the bottle of tequila. I sit on the couch crafting a new Facebook page for her. The tequila warms my skin and I feel uncomfortable in my dress clothes. Carla sits next to me, hovering over my shoulder. Her breath smells faintly tart, like the tequila. "Why are you making another one of those?"

"So you have a political account. It's different."

The heat of her body bleeds through her shirt. She sweats lightly. So do I—my skin feels glued into my jeans and my brand-new blouse sticks to the small of my back. "Miles tried to teach me how to do that on the phone," she says. Her eyes flicker to the picture on the wall, then away. "I don't understand Facebook."

I finish typing and save the page. "Do you miss him?"

"Most of the time."

"And his dad is helping out?"

She hesitates. "I don't need him to."

I turn so we're face to face and my gaze goes to her lips. They're wet with alcohol, her face flushed. She breathes loudly. There's vulnerability in her blue eyes and it gets to me, deep down in my belly. I reach out and remove a lock of hair from her face, tuck it behind her ear. Her breath hitches. I've done this a million times before, but this time I linger a little bit longer, watching her breath, suddenly out of control. I imagine what it would be like to run my knuckles across her neck, over the checkered scar on the ridge of her jawline.

She swallows and her eyes flutter shut.

I've thought about fucking Carla on and off for a long time. I've imagined doing her in my apartment, or pulled over on the side of Route 1 on the way home. But it's never been like this.

Her phone rings.

She startles, pulls away, and I feel like punting the phone out of the room. "It's Miles," she says. "I have to take this." She tilts away from me when she answers the phone and I fight the brief feeling of anger that floods my body. "Hey, baby. You okay?"

I can hear his voice through the phone, calm, not panicked. A college kid who doesn't realize what a 10:30 pm call home might seem like.

A buzzing sensation nips at the back of my skull. I turn the laptop off, start packing it up. Night streams in through the windows. The heat of the day has receded and now a breeze pushes in through the windows. I watch Carla's face as she speaks to her son. Her mouth twists, revealing a slightly crooked canine tooth.

French speakers have a saying for what Carla is. I picked up the term in Montserrat when I was little. *Jolie laide*. It means pretty and ugly. The kind of woman that is beautiful because of her charisma and the way she holds herself. The kind of woman you can't stop staring at, but you don't know why. Unexpectedly attractive.

I stand just as Carla says, "I love you. Be safe."

The sound of the clock ticking on the wall fills the room.

"Eli…" she says.

"He okay?"

"He's fine." She makes a face. "I think he'd been drinking, actually."

I turn to look at her. She's short and stocky and perfect. With the alcohol in my system, I just want to run my hands over her

8

curves. I want the smell of her shampoo on me and the sound of her breath in my ear. But she doesn't need me. She doesn't need anybody. "I'm going to write up the press release on Monday and send it out. Tell Miles to be a good boy for the next few months."

She idles and the smell of grease and meat and salt hangs in the air. Carla isn't a great cook but she's not terrible, either. So much of her is like that; a good Samaritan, but not a great one. Composed but not elegant. Sharp, but not exceptionally intelligent.

Without saying anything else, I turn and head for the door. Carla shuffles behind me. My heart still races from being so close to her but another feeling bubbles in me now, too. Something deeper. Darker.

On the front steps she says, "Please be careful driving home."

"I'm fine," I say.

"I hate you drinking and driving."

I hesitate and the heat of the Keys piles in—the thickness of the air, even in the summer. The sound of the crickets and smell of the mangroves, like bacteria and sea grass, the prime of the earth.

I want to stay. I do. But it doesn't feel right. There's still so much hesitation in me, like I'm missing something. Why is she being so nice? She doesn't need me.

"Don't worry about my drinking," I say.

"Well, I do."

"Carla..."

She makes a face, and for a moment, her body tenses. "It's fine," she says. "Text me when you get home."

In the florescent lighting, her skin looks faintly yellow. I imagine pressing my palms to the freckles on her neck, feeling the erratic beat of her pulse against mine. I wonder if she's dizzy, if she's drunk. What she'll feel like tomorrow, if she'll think of me when she wakes up.

TWO

Carla wakes up at four am with a hangover. Her mouth feels like sandpaper, and nausea tugs on the pit of her stomach. Dryness spreads along the back of her skull. It's been months, maybe longer, since she drank this much. She rises from the bed. This close to fifty, she really can't be drinking anymore.

She pads into the kitchen, rustling a stack of papers on the floor. She feels heavy, old. In the kitchen, she pours herself a giant glass of water and takes three Advil. After the first couple of sips of water, she feels better. But her body is still restless and overheated, so she stands there for a while, looking out at the table where she sat earlier, Eli by her side.

Moonlight spills in from the uncovered window, painting the kitchen a misty grey as she sips and thinks about dinner. Eli's hand on her hair. It's happened before but this time it felt different, like diving into a pool for the first time. It hit her hard.

She exhales, watching the moon filter through the window.

She just had one too many glasses of tequila. Eli is a good-looking woman, lean and tall with just a hint of something masculine in her stature. She's funny and quick and smarter than just about everyone else in the Keys.

Carla leans back against the countertop. It pushes into her back, her ass. She's gained ten pounds in the last year. Jeb, her on-again off-again boyfriend, has been on her to lose the weight. But it's the cigarettes. She can't stop eating now that she's no longer smoking.

Clouds rush in over the moon, dampening the light. The kitchen falls into darkness for a brief moment. Then the clouds pass. It lightens again. She refills her drink and heads back to the bedroom.

She has to keep focused on the election, not Eli. The election is what matters. This town needs fiscal responsibility. They could use her help. Plus, she needs to clean up the streets. Too many homeless. Too many illegal immigrants.

This will be good for her and everyone else. She just has to focus.

The moment last night was just a fluke. They would never work together. Carla is too old. Things are just different for her generation. It was nice to be wanted, but she knows better. It won't happen again.

•••

Carla wakes up after the sun has risen to a text from Miles.

sorry I called so late mama. love you

She smiles and holds the phone to her chest for a moment, then places it on the nightstand. It's almost eight in the morning. Saturday. Usually, she catches up on finances Saturday mornings. Today she feels like staying in her pajamas, having a Bloody Mary, and watching a movie.

So she does. She pulls the curtains over the windows and sits down on the couch to watch The Notebook. She feels tired inside her body, like she hasn't in a long time. Probably excitement over the campaign. Curled into a blanket on the couch, she watches Ryan Gosling scoop Rachel McAdams into his arms.

There's something about Rachel McAdams that's always rubbed her the wrong way. She looks like a girl from school, Mary. Mary was cute, small. She was prom queen. She volunteered at the food bank. She used to hold Carla down in the back of the school bus and she and her friends would take turns kicking her.

Carla exhales as a chill races through her body. She takes another sip of the Bloody Mary, shuffles deeper into the covers.

Her mind goes to Eli, her voice, the corded muscles in her arms and the way she's so quiet sometimes, and so forward other times, mischievous almost. She's not sure where she got the idea to have Eli be her campaign manager. It just came to her in the middle of the day. She wanted someone who would make her laugh. Someone with no fear. Someone who would give her everything.

Carla rises and goes to the kitchen where she makes a skillet full of bacon. The smell of grease wafts through the apartment. This will help her hangover. Get her in the right frame of mind.

Carla brews a pot of coffee and stares out the window above the sink. She wonders what Eli is doing. If she's hungover or if she's sleeping. If she's going to the Business Guild benefit concert later. A sudden heat settles in her belly and she forces herself to think about other things.

•••

Jeb surprises her by showing up at the house as she's leaving for the benefit concert. She's feeling better by then, less tired and the Bloody Mary and bacon have cured her hangover. Still, her muscles tense at the sight of him.

"I didn't know you were coming," she says.

He stands in the doorway while she puts on her sneakers. He wears a long sleeved white shirt and jeans, large boots with a bandana tied around his neck and Trump hat. He dresses like a redneck even though he has more money than the millionaires on Duck Key. She hates it. And he gets away with it because he's a Conch, a native of the Keys. Everyone knows him and his family. People invite him to everything. He can do no wrong, even pissing in front of the Green Parrot during a Jimmy Buffet concert.

"I need a ride downtown," he says. "And I thought you could use some company."

"Not really."

He makes a face, staring down at her as she struggles to get on her last sneaker. "Well shit, Carla."

Carla rises. He smells like diesel. "It's fine. Are you drinking tonight? Who's going to bring you back to get your car?"

"Tommy."

She stands. She's in jeans and a t-shirt today. It's hot and over-cast and she's pretty sure the ground will be wet. Everything's been saturated for weeks. The rain's let up but it's in the air—hanging there. Stagnant. She hates this kind of weather.

"That okay, babe?"

She reaches around him to grab her purse but he moves so he blocks it with his body. Then he stoops down and gives her a peck on the mouth. She stops, flustered, and touches his shoulder. "Sorry." She pecks him back. "That's fine. Thank you for coming with me."

Jeb opens the door and steps out onto the porch with his back to her. "You ever pick someone to do all that campaign crap for you?"

Carla locks the door, pulls her sunglasses down over her eyes. "Not really." The muscles around her mouth tighten. Jeb doesn't need to know yet; she doesn't want to deal with his complaining. Eli is gay, yes. She's a dem, yes. But she's smart. Sharp. Carla needs someone like that. "I don't know. I haven't decided for sure yet."

"My buddy Jimmy in Marathon could help."

"I don't know him that well," she says. "But thanks."

She makes her way to the car, feeling the mist on her arms. It sends a shiver through her body. She thinks about dinner last night and the way Eli reached out so brazenly, tucking her hair behind her ear. Her cheeks heat.

"What?" Jeb says.

She turns to look at him. "What do you mean, what?"

"You're smiling."

She forces a frown, looks away from him. Irritation wells in her mouth as she climbs into the driver's seat. She locks the door and starts the engine, pushing the thoughts away. They won't do her any good. She's felt like this for the longest time—like being at the bottom of a boat anchor. Ocean pressing around on her. There's nothing she can do to get it to go away.

THREE

The next morning I'm dry headed and undone, like my seams are splitting open and my guts are about to fall out. The elderly couple that owns my house has returned from a week-long trip to Aruba and their angry voices wake me. Rubbing my forehead, I make my way to the refrigerator and gulp orange juice straight from the container, spilling dribbles onto my shirt. The apartment still reeks of sage.

I shower. In the spray, I close my eyes and let the water sting my scalp, rinsing conditioner out of my hair. I imagine Carla's face—the freckles, the top tooth slightly crooked. I picture her hair, the curve of her hips, her ass.

My hand inadvertently slips over one nipple. I lean forward, resting the other hand against the wall behind the showerhead. As I've gotten older, my boobs have grown fuller and my stomach is still tight, but not flat like it was in high school.

At eighteen, I was stick skinny. I had no boobs. Long, thick blonde hair, all bones and angles at five-nine. My girlfriend back then was a thirty-five-year-old named Yaurena. She was heavier than me, but barely, with dark hair and tan skin. She had a husband, too, one that was frequently gone on long trips.

Seven months into our relationship, he got a job in California and they moved.

Yaurena was the first and only girlfriend I've ever had. I learned from her how to spend long periods of time with someone, how to anticipate needs, how to please. She showed me how easy it is to become obsessed.

My chest tightens. Pinpricks of pain radiate out. I rub my chest until they subside, then turn the showerhead off and towel dry.

It's two pm by the time I get to the Business Guild concert and although the weather is perfect for a Saturday afternoon in the Keys, it's much hotter than it should be.

The concert is being held at Fort East Martello, a park that's overlooked by the airport and a tall tower-like fort made of brick. A bunch of us from the Guild volunteer selling food and drinks. Across the street, the ocean slaps at a thick wall of concrete. It smells of seagrass and salt. I take my wedges off to walk to the mixed drinks booth I'll be volunteering at all night. Light amber rum from the local distillery lines the sides of it.

"Calvin, please tell me you have something decent in your booth."

The man behind the beer booth next to me smiles, throwing over a can of Blue Moon. He's tall, but heavy, and has a genial face—a guy with average intelligence who doesn't push his luck in the world. When I open the Blue Moon, beer foam fizzles across my fingers. I lick them off before pulling the ice chest closer and arrange the drink mixers. That's when I spot Carla entering the park.

She wears jeans and a Guild t-shirt—black with a flamboyant rainbow across her breasts. I stifle a laugh. Then I see the person following behind her and stop. Jeb. He follows Carla to the main ticketing booth in a *Make America Great Again* hat. A native Conch, everyone knows him and wants to be friends with him, even though he's a drunk who smells like wet cigarettes. That's what money and history do for people down here, even losers.

"Calvin, do you think I'm pretty?"

Calvin makes a face. "Yeah, you're pretty. But you eat pussy. Don't you?"

A smile creeps over my lips. Of course he thinks I'm pretty. Stupid boys always think I'm pretty. "How's your wife?"

"Oh, she's fine," Calvin says. "Don't get any ideas, though."

I laugh. I like Calvin. He's one of the younger guys in the Rotary Club—in his mid-forties and balding. He's also one of the few people in this town I would ever consider being friends with. Most people here aren't trustworthy. Besides a couple guys at my gym, I don't hang out with pretty much anyone.

By four pm, most of the concert-goers have arrived and Jeb is long gone. Carla has taken charge of the volunteers and barks orders. She's different in public. More forceful. Her guard is up.

I want her to drop by but she stays at her booth as more attendees pour in and the band starts. Country music. Fucking figures. Carla sports sneakers today and when it starts to mist, they grow brown with the mud. It's still warm and the mist only lasts for a little while, then people start lining up at my booth in droves. I get a two-hundred-dollar tip. A very drunk man asks me to marry him.

After a while, I get tired. I drink my own mixed drink, a rum on ice. I run out of cranberry juice. I get buzzed. Humid air settles on my skin in a dense grid.

It seems like it's been hours when the concert finally stops, and I start putting away the remaining liquor bottles. I open the ice chest and knock it open over the ground so it will melt. My fingers are still cold from scooping the little cubes with the plastic cups.

Finally, Carla makes her way over to the booth. She looks tired, but her eyes aren't the way they usually are. They're more focused, sturdy. I'm irritated that it took so long for her to come over, that she didn't tell me she's back with Jeb. I reach for the bottle of rum only to knock it over. It's empty anyway. "Go get something to eat, Eli."

I prop the empty bottle back up. "Take your pants off and come on over here."

A blush flushes her face. "You're drunk."

"I'm fine."

"Who's driving you home?"

I smile. "You are."

Carla exhales and turns like she's looking for someone, but Jeb isn't there anymore. It's just the rapidly cooling night around us, the smell of marijuana and the slick blades of grass. Finally, she turns back to me. Faint perspiration stains the top of her shirt and her hair curls damp around her skin. "Angel will drive you," she says. "He lives in Big Coppitt, too."

I stare at her. "I want you to drive me."

"Let me get him."

"Either you drive me, or I'm driving myself."

Carla glares. "You're being immature."

I force a laugh as anger swells in my chest. Carla is always telling me how young I am. How immature and inexperienced. She acts like it's something that makes her better than me, or can keep us away from one another.

I think about how I felt as a kid, finding out Mom had left. I think about the volcano, and immigrating to Miami with close to nothing. Watching Dad lose over eighty pounds during chemo treatments when I was finishing high school. How hard it was when Yaurena left. I laugh again. "My bad," I say. "Why don't you go on and tell Angel to come over here."

· · ·

I'm heading across the parking lot gravel to Angel's car when Carla comes hustling after me. She barrels, small and busty and furious, all of the things I love most about her. "I'm leaving," she says. "Get in the car if you want. I don't care."

Before last night, I was happy to see her at luncheons, flirt harmlessly, buy her drinks at happy hours and let my hand linger on the small of her back. But something feels different now. Maybe it's the heat of the season. Maybe it's because I've finally been in her house and seen how cramped it was, and at the same time, how empty, and how it feels like suddenly she could need me.

I trail her to the car and slide in the passenger's seat. Heels with broken insoles lay flat on the floor, along with a bag full of papers. It smells like new car, even though I know she's had this model for at least a year now. I stare at her thighs, the way they curve in those jeans.

"I've been thinking," I say. We hang a right, moving through the triangle and out of Key West. "You'll need to redo your professional pictures."

Carla is silent for a moment before shifting in her seat. She's funny about pictures. Won't take them, won't post them on Facebook if she's in them. Part of me knows she really does need new ones but part of me just delights in the terror that sweeps her face. "Why?"

"Your most recent ones are five years old."

She glances at me, then back at the road. Sweat dries around her hairline. She looks older, haggard. "So?"

"So you look different now."

"Yeah, I'm fat now."

She blinks several times, steers the car to turn with the curve. A tightness springs up in my throat. I place my hand on her thigh. She doesn't move but her breathing speeds up. The heat of her body bleeds through the jeans. "You're perfect."

"Oh God," she says. "Give me a break."

It's quiet for several moments, only the hum of the tires on the pavement and the soft tinkle of the radio. I remove my hand. "You have to take them. You know you do."

She exhales. "I know, but not now."

"Yes, now. The signs have to be done early."

I stare at her. I know I should stop. I want to. But then I think about Jeb. He pissed on the side of the Green Parrot once. He wears camo, doesn't shave. I look down at her waist and the way her hips curve. Carla is beautiful. Perfect and much too good for him. I've always thought so.

"Fine," she says eventually. "Schedule something for a morning. I book up afternoons."

We drive in silence for the rest of the ride. She drops me at the house, refusing to come inside for a glass of water. She leaves quickly and in the darkness, I can barely see her taillights as she heads back to the main road. Under a spread of stars, I stand out on the porch and look out across the key. The lamplights glimmer on route one, but otherwise there's not much else.

I picture her car weaving around corners, accelerating over bridges. I imagine her thinking of me as she's driving, and nestling her hand between her legs for relief.

FOUR

Carla prickles with sweat. She stands outside on the back porch of her house overlooking the canal, posing for the photo Eli will use for the campaign. The sun beams down on an angle—still fledgling in the sky—it's barely eight o'clock. She normally doesn't start working until nine or ten and the tailored suit jacket feels uncomfortable, too tight. She's a furnace. Always has been.

"Carla, tilt your head a little." The female photographer, probably one of Eli's gay friends, moves her finger through the air, guiding Carla's gaze. She follows it, feeling stupid. Behind, water laps at the unused dock. The air is quiet. "There we go. Now try smiling, please."

She tries smiling close-lipped but it feels wrong, like she's forcing it. Someone sniggers from the corner and Carla abruptly turns to face Eli. "You try it," she snaps. "I didn't even want to do this in the first place."

Eli stands, her back pressed to the side of the house. She's in skin tight pants and collared blouse, an outfit Carla could never get away with wearing. Her light hair is tied up in a bun. She looks good. As usual. "Meg," Eli says to the photographer, "take a five-minute break."

Meg nods and checks the camera. A breeze sweeps off the ocean, smelling of salt and sulphur. Carla stands and peels off the stupid suit jacket, exhaling at the feel of the air on her bare arms.

"Come inside," Eli says.

Carla's stomach lurches. She follows Eli inside and watches as she mixes a mimosa, strong, then holds it out. "It's eight in the morning," Carla says. She feels like a bitch. She doesn't care.

"Drink."

Heat flickers across Carla's skin. She's afraid Eli will see the blush so she takes the mimosa and gulps it back all at once. Eli wouldn't balk, so she shouldn't either. And it's not a bad choice; smooth, bubbling orange juice cools her mouth, her throat. She hadn't realized how thirsty she was.

"What's the issue?"

Carla goes to the refrigerator and refills the champagne, only adding a hint of orange juice. "There are more important things we could be doing."

"Your signs and your presence at social events are the two most important things to winning an election."

Carla drinks more. It's unlike her. Day drinking is for people without jobs.

"You're uncomfortable," Eli says. A hint of a smile touches her lips. She moves closer, reaches out, tucks a strand of hair behind Carla's ear. "Tell me."

Goosebumps race up her spine. She rubs the lip of the champagne glass. "I don't like having my picture taken."

Eli hesitates and something like electricity races through Carla's stomach, all the way down to her thighs. She clenches them. Focus, she tells herself. Don't be an idiot.

"Sometimes we do things because they need to be done," Eli says. "You know that better than anybody else."

The hum of the alcohol settles deep in her belly. Her blood buzzes. She feels too fat and too old to be taking pictures with the most in-your-face gay woman in town. She should've hired someone else to run her campaign. She could've, but she didn't want to.

• • •

After Eli and the photographer leave, Carla grabs her things and finally gets to the office around noon. She sweats like a hog by the time she sits down at her desk and starts sorting emails.

She's starving. And irritated. Sun pours in through the windows.

After several minutes, she stands and closes the blinds. Fanning out her blouse, she opens the door and heads into the office kitchen. A turkey sandwich from yesterday sits on the third row of the refrigerator. She grabs it and puts it in the toaster oven, then pours herself a large glass of water.

"Hey, Carla."

Carla turns. One of the younger real estate agents in the office stands behind her. She's small, skinny like Eli is. But this girl is fake, always running her mouth. Carla hates the bitch. "Marjory."

"Heard the big news."

"What's that?"

Marjory smiles but it looks more like a grimace. "The election," she says. "Heard you're running for city mayor."

"Right."

The toaster zings. Carla removes the sandwich from inside and puts it on a plate. Then she goes to the refrigerator and pulls out a can of mayonnaise to put on the bread. Marjory moves around behind her, assembling her lunch. A guacamole salad. Carla rolls her eyes. "Read your press release," Marjory continues, "You know, I know your campaign manager."

"A lot of people know Eli."

"I went to high school with her."

Carla falls silent, smearing the mayonnaise. She's fat. She doesn't need this much mayo. She probably shouldn't eat anything for another month considering how much weight she wants to lose. "That's great."

"I was two grades ahead of her. No one really liked her."

Heat licks Carla's skull. She stops with the mayonnaise. The smell of it turns her stomach and for a moment she breathes the other direction. "Eli probably didn't like any of you, either." She tosses the knife in the sink with a clang. Louder than she meant. When she looks up, Marjory stares at her. She clasps one hand around a fork and the other holds the bowl.

"She basically jumped off the top of someone's truck into a swimming pool one time. She's like crazy. Right?"

"Do you always have to be such a bitch?" Carla snaps. The room goes silent. Carla's chest grows warm, and her cheeks soon after. She closes her eyes, turns away from Marjory. Waning sparks shoot through her body. She feels blindsided. Where did that come from? "Sorry," she finally says. "It's been a long day already."

Marjory's quiet, sprinkling pepper over her stupid avocado and lettuce. She puts the pepper shaker back on the counter and walks out without saying another word.

•••

Carla eats in silence, washes her hands, and goes back to her office. It's quiet inside. She feels better now that she's eaten but there's something else. Like pinpricks on her hands and kneecaps. She's just starting to draw up a contact when the lights flicker out. Her computer goes dead. Landline, too.

"Goddammnit."

She stands and goes to the window. Lights are out in the supermarket next door and the car repair garage—probably whole area's out. Normal for the Keys. She's been here for almost twenty years and the random power outages have persisted. She picks her phone up off the desk.

you have power?

She waits. Then Eli texts *Fine on Stock Island. You okay?*

fine

Several seconds pass. Then: *Need me to come rescue you?*

Carla smiles and warmth swells through her body. That's why she likes Eli, because she's funny. She's smart, too. And capable. It's caught her off guard how much she likes Eli. How much she thinks about her.

Whatever Carla texts back. *I'm fine*

Sure you are. Call if you need anything.

Carla puts her phone down. Several minutes later the power comes back on and she's able to finish up that contract on Ramrod Key. When she's done, she picks her phone up again. She's still warm but not overheated like before. She opens the text thread and looks down at the conversation. Seeing it again makes her smile.

FIVE

My mother disappeared when I was five years old. We woke up one day and she was gone. At that time, Mimi, Dad, and I all lived in the same house in Monserrat, a two-story stilt home just east of Plymouth, close to the Soufriere Hills where the volcano was. Mimi lived on the top floor and my parents had a bedroom on the west end. My bed was in my dad's old office, on the east, facing the hills. I woke up that morning to a sea of green, the hills like pyramids towering over me.

By this time, Mom had gotten deep into drugs. When my father was at work in downtown Plymouth, she'd scream at me and Mimi and leave the house in fits of rage. I wished her gone a million times. I liked the quiet of the house better when it was just me and Mimi.

"Now listen," Mimi said, taking me by the shoulders. Dad had already left for work. "Your mum wasn't here this morning when we woke up."

I stared at her, calm. "She will come back," I said.

Mimi's hands stayed on my shoulders. "We don't know where she went this time."

Outside the house, a swallow cooed. I'd learned all the bird names and memorized how they looked. I watched them soar outside my bedroom window when Mom yelled.

"Are you alright, pet? Mimi is still here."

I put my hands on the sides of Mimi's face. She was pale, with bright green eyes and white blonde hair. Locals thought she was Dutch or Polish. Much of her beauty came from her calm. It was deep rooted, something that emanated from within her. I was the opposite—my eyes were restless, she said. "Do you want me to make her come back?" I lay my forehead against hers. "Do you want me to, Mimi?"

Her body stiffened. Then she took my hands from her face and kissed them, rose from her chair, and went to do her daily incantations.

•••

Meg is quick on the turnaround and I receive proofs from Carla's photoshoot in less than twenty-four hours. They're stunning. They pull at something inside me that I haven't felt since living in Montserrat.

I call Carla and we sit in her office in New Town, reviewing them. She wears her normal work attire—a satin blouse and pants, her newly pedicured toes poking out from red wedges. I'm not a huge fan of her feet. They're too fat, and always stuffed into the point of a wedge or heel.

"Do you really expect me to pick one of these?"

Someone in the office has just microwaved lasagna and the smell of marinara sauce blooms throughout the space. Carla wrinkles her nose. She puts a hand over the prints and her gaze goes soft, wrinkles creasing around her eyes. It makes her look like a child.

"They don't look like me."

"They're professional photos," I say. Granted, some of them don't look like she does day by day, but there are a few that really capture what's attractive about her—her eyes and her thick, beautiful curls. "They look amazing. You just don't like pictures of yourself."

Carla gazes down at the prints.

What I haven't shown her are the photos at the beginning of the shoot, just after she had the mimosa. Her eyes are dark, full of want and fire in a way I have never seen them before. She's looking slightly off-camera. At me.

"This one's okay." She points to a seated shot of her gazing sweetly up at the camera.

"What about this one?" I push forward a shot of her standing at the edge of the porch, her eyes stronger, more focused and steely. She looks slender, too, which is why I know she'll give me the okay to use it.

"Fine," she says.

She shifts in her seat. Today she wears a blouse that's uncharacteristically low cut for her. I can see the full shape of her breasts in it. She has a really nice rack, especially for someone of her age who's had a kid. They're still full and firm, more long than round, and smooth, dotted with light freckles like the rest of her. She catches me staring and pulls the top up.

I lean forward over her desk. "Are you okay for me to go ahead with the signs?"

Her eyes flicker over me. "Yes."

She sits quiet today, meek. It's not like her at all. I reach out and touch her hand. She looks down at it, then back up at me. Her hair is still perfect from the shoot—large and round and coiled loosely about her shoulders. "What's wrong, Carla?"

She exhales.

"What?"

She looks down at the pictures and something inside me breaks. I knew she was self-conscious, but not like this. It makes me feel like taking her into my arms and kissing her cheeks and telling her how perfect and beautiful and strong she is. "Nothing." Her eyes water when I pass my hand over hers. "I'm fine."

Her necklace bobs between her breasts, a small gold sailboat. "Stop thinking about the pictures," I say. "Think about what you're going to do when you win."

She meets my eyes and some of that steeliness returns. It still feels so different than it did a week ago, before all this. It feels like we are moving forward too quickly somehow. Like I'm doing something wrong. "I know," she says. "I'm fine, Eli."

SIX

Carla can't sleep the next night. A storm flickers the electricity several times. The house shakes with booms of thunder. She gets up and paces, cleaning up the old accordion files and stuffing things inside her desk and in the closet in her office. She opens the windows and airs the house out. She throws away the leftover meatloaf.

After the brunt of the storm passes, she lies down to sleep three different times but anxiety boils inside her chest, keeping her awake. She's been careful to keep people from knowing how severe her panic attacks are. Sometimes they're so bad she can barely function. At work, she locks the door and sits down on the floor, crying as quietly as possible until they pass. She mentioned them once to Jeb. Once to Eli when things got really bad.

"Can't you just take an Ativan or somethin'?" Jeb muttered. "Seems silly to lose a day of work over that."

Eli said that a lot of people get them. That it was nothing to hide.

Now, lying in bed looking up at the ceiling, she watches the moonlight shift across the walls as the clouds change. It reminds her of the way the sky changed at her father's house in upstate New York. They moved there when she was in grade school. She had no friends and all the girls picked on her for wearing long dresses and refusing to touch a cigarette.

Carla rolls over in bed and smooths her hand across the empty pillow next to her. She could win this election. She should. With the current mayor's sex scandal and the crazy frat boy running against her, she makes a good opponent. A great one. Everything will be fine. She managed when her ex-husband cheated on her and disappeared with a younger woman. She managed to raise her kid alone in the Keys without a pointless college degree. She worked instead of playing around like most college kids. She didn't have the luxury.

Car headlights roll across her window, sending waves of shadows across the room before it falls into darkness again. Carla thinks of Eli, then. The way she smiles, the way she stands, the way she treats her like a God. No one has ever paid attention to her like that before.

Something warm twinges deep within her belly.

She shifts positions, crossing and uncrossing her legs, but there's nothing she can do to get rid of the feeling.

SEVEN

I can't sleep. It storms, hard. The electricity goes off twice as winds batter the side of the house. Thunder booms. Even with the curtains closed, the flashes of lightning light up my room.

Around four am, I finally get up. My mouth is dry so I suck down an Orangina before turning up the central air. The breeze whispers across my arms. There's next to no air flow up here with the windows shut, and the whole place feels stale and dank.

I think of Mimi and how she sometimes played with candles at night while the house slept. Dad called it her "voodoo."

I throw the Orangina bottle in the recycling bin. It makes a tinny clang against the sides and I keep thinking about the way Carla looked at me after drinking those two mimosas. Like she was going to stalk me and burn my house down.

After a couple of minutes, I gather some things on the kitchen table. I have that dry buzzing sensation at the back of my skull— the kind you get after not sleeping enough, or having one too many tequila shots. I place a soy pillar candle and some patchouli inside a glass cylinder. I grab one of the proofs of Carla, a candid shot where she's looking at me and not the camera, and hold one of Mimi's old quartz crystals in my left palm. Then I light the candle. As the heat inside the cylinder grows, the smell of patchouli filters out.

I don't really know what I'm doing. My body just moves of its own accord—things I've seen Mimi do. Rituals that are like second nature.

It's dark out and the haze of smoke fogs the room up even more. I'm lightheaded. Something electric gurgles in my stomach. I feel like I did before the volcano in Montserrat—I'll always remember the sensation, the way my stomach seemed like it was crawling down into my ass.

I focus on the candle, the flickering flame, and exhale slowly. I wave my hand over it, dispensing the scent of burning plastic and smoke. Then I pick up the picture of Carla and hold it over the flame. I think of her face and neck, her hips and ass.

Slowly, I dip the picture into the heat. The edges of the proof start to curl and burn, growing tan, then black, and whispering trails of smoke. I focus in on the feeling, the image of her, until the entire picture has burns and small tendrils of fire burn my fingertips.

● ● ●

I go back to sleep for two hours, and when I wake up, I'm exhausted. My temples throb. I have to drag myself through the kitchen and drink half a quart of orange juice. The coolness of the juice on my throat helps somewhat but there's still the pain in my head.

I nibble on some Gouda cheese and reach for the phone, dialing Mimi's number from memory. The clouds from last night have cleared but a grey sheen still hangs in the air. The sea water thrashes at the mangroves along the rim of the Key, spitting white surfs.

"Eliza?" Mimi answers. "What is wrong? You sound heavy."

I swallow a huge chunk of cheese, picturing her in her condominium, only a few blocks from the mall, sitting in her rocking chair with a large spun sweater clumped over her small shoulders. Probably smoking.

"You are in love," she states finally.

I smirk. "That is some powerful voodoo, Mimi."

"You always call me when you are lovesick."

I place the Gouda back inside the refrigerator. It has a smell to it, like it was off for a little too long last night when the power went out. "This is different," I say. "Maybe I should work some magic on her and make her fall in love with me."

"Not smart."

"Why?"

"Because this comes from a place of darkness, pet."

I roll my eyes and bring the candle cylinder to the sink to wash out. "That's a good thing," I say, wedging the phone between my ear and my shoulder. "It means the underworld gods will hear my pleas."

Through the phone, Mimi huffs. It's silent for a moment, and then the switch of a lighter fills the line. She inhales, exhales. I can almost smell the smoke from over two hundred miles away.

"What is so wrong with wanting someone?"

"I know what you want," she says. "You cannot make people love you."

Pain expands inside my chest, the warm kind. It burns. It's the kind I get at night when I'm at home alone and have to remind myself that loneliness can't kill me. I touch my chest and make a fist with my hand. For a moment, I consider telling her about what I did last night, but then reconsider. It was only playing. I was tired and wanted to feel in control.

I'm nothing like Mimi. I can't even get this headache to pass.

• • •

That day at work, everything feels the same except I'm sick. No matter how much Tylenol I take, the tension in my head remains. I manage to get through a meeting with a big client at Tavern N Town but by four pm, I'm exhausted, shaky, and on the verge of crying during the drive home.

Mangroves and palm trees blur past me. It's another unusually warm day but there's something cold in the breeze, maybe indicating an oncoming cold front, and I breathe the air in deep gulps. I'm irritated for being sick when I have so much work to do. That's when my phone lights up. I glance over to see Carla's name and message on the screen.

lucille invited me to the first open candidates forum in a month

I turn down my road. Rocks along the side of the road kick up under my car, rattling the undercarriage. I press on the gas and take the turn into my driveway too fast. Even though it's only four-thirty, the sun is low on the horizon, peeking over the azalea bushes, their bushy twigs knotted together, leaves budding with early spring flowers. The breeze here smells like salt and fish, like dirty sand.

I park and head upstairs to my apartment, opening all the windows to let the breeze in. I light a lavender candle, drink an entire bottle of cranberry juice, and lie down on the couch.

My phone vibrates.

what should I tell her

I pick it up but the light hurts. I feel like there is smoke inside of me, pressing against my eyes and mouth. *Sick.* I text her back.

My phone is still for several seconds, then vibrates again. *sick how? bad?*

I text back, *Bad.*

Then I lay my head back on the couch cushion, feeling the whir of the salted breeze pass over me. I want Carla more than just about anything, but I want more to not feel like this anymore. Exhaling, I close my eyes.

EIGHT

Eli has always been dramatic. She gestures wildly when she talks and gets upset over unimportant things, like car trouble and credit card payments. That's why Carla's not sure what to do when Eli texts that she's sick.

She tries texting again but Eli doesn't reply. She calls. Nothing.

It's a nice afternoon, sunny with some clouds, but the wind feels different. Maybe a cold front coming. At five pm, Carla packs up her things and leaves work, heading for Eli's house in Big Coppitt. Her palms are sweaty as she makes the turn and parks beneath the house. Sparks fire in the pit of her belly. More and more now when she's going to meet up with Eli, she gets these nerves.

A breeze ferries under the house as she gets out of the car, nipping at the hems of her pants. Her sandals wobble on the rock. She climbs the wood stairs to the third floor and knocks once. No answer. She tries the doorknob. It's open. When she steps inside, she smells lavender and finds Eli curled up on the couch. The windows are open, pouring in cool breeze. Eli's skin flushes, her eyes squeezed shut.

Carla goes immediately to the kitchen and pours a glass of water. She then scours the medicine cabinet in the bathroom, takes three Tylenols out of a small bottle, and returns to the living room. "Eli?" She sits on the couch, tilting Eli's face up.

Eli's skin is hot and her pulse races. For a moment, Carla gets scared. Scared like she got when Miles took a hit in lacrosse his junior year and stayed down on the field too long. Scared like when her father fell on ice last year. But then Eli opens her eyes and says, "Hi, beautiful."

Carla holds out the Tylenols and water. "Take these."

"I took some already."

"Drink the water, then."

Eli takes the glass of water and brings it to her lips. She sips once, then places the glass back in Carla's hands. Dark circles rim her eyes. She looks like those homeless people that line the front of the food pantry in the morning. Desperate. Needing. Frustration tugs on Carla but there's another feeling, too—a fire in the base of her belly. "You need to be in bed, resting."

"I was resting until you showed up."

Carla sighs. "Get in bed. Now."

A shadow sweeps over Eli's face. She frowns, then leans forward and pushes into a standing position. Carla follows her to the bedroom. The room is small. There's barely any privacy with the half wall, and there's not a lot of furniture, either. Just the bed and a nightstand, the closet in the corner. A painting of a naked woman hangs on the western wall. It's a bachelor's pad. She should've known.

Carla moves toward the nightstand when Eli starts to strip off her pants. She stops, water in hand. "Eli?"

One pant leg tangles around Eli's foot. She kicks it off.

After climbing out of her pants, she strips off her shirt and tosses it to the floor. Her muscles are well defined without being bulky. A thin line ridges her back. Her thighs are the same, curving gently like her calves.

Carla's neck grows hot and she looks away. But then Eli unhooks the clasp of her bra and she can't not look. She keeps her eyes there, even when Eli turns. Her stomach is flat. Her breasts are small but pert. She looks more athletic without clothes, strong and comfortable with herself in a way Carla could never be.

"Bring me the water," Eli says.

For a second, Carla just stands there, heat rippling through her body. Then she moves forward, placing the glass back in Eli's hands. "Rest," she manages to say, but her voice is tight and tense and it springs another blush to her cheeks.

NINE

My fever rages until around two am. Carla has stayed and by this point, she demands I take a cold shower. She aims the spray directly on me as I sit on the floor of the tub, resting my head on my arms.

I break into gooseflesh when she smooths the water down my back, squeezing long rivulets from my hair. My nipples harden but I don't make any effort to cover them. I have nice boobs. Too bad she's seeing them for the first time like this.

"Fever's dropping," I say.

Carla places her hand on my back. Water splashes the floor, the shirt she borrowed, soaking up into the bath mat and her pants. "It was so high for so long."

Gooseflesh again. Although I feel somewhat better than I did this afternoon, my head still pounds. I grab Carla's hand and bring it to my chest, hold it there. She stares at me. Her eyes have that open look they get when she's concerned—her brows knit together, small wrinkles forming over the bridge of her nose.

"Come on," she says.

She turns off the spray and grabs a towel from behind her. I imagine her doing this with her father when he got sick several months ago, doing this with Miles when he was a child. Her hair hangs limp over her shoulders but she seems calm, like she knows what to do. It's in this moment that I find her most attractive. Carla has the unnerving ability to take care of things, to get things done even if she doesn't like them, even if they are difficult.

I dry quickly and slip into a long t-shirt. I'm still weak. I can feel the sickness in my joints as I lie back down on the bed. Carla lies down next to me so we're face to face, on our sides. It's unlike her but I don't care. Her eyes are alight, her hair slipping over her shoulders.

"Are you tired?" I ask. She's quiet. Just staring. Lying like this, her anchor necklace dips into her cleavage. I reach out and touch the gold pendant; it's warm and smooth. Her breathing quickens. "Sleep," I tell her.

Her chest rises and falls. Her gaze meets mine and holds there.

• • •

By daybreak, Carla is gone. I'm disappointed somehow, but I don't know why. I shouldn't have expected her to stay. It was unlike her to even show up at all.

My fever is gone. My body is tired but doesn't ache like it did before. I finally get up around ten am and begin working. The house is muted, silent in what seems to be an oncoming cold front. I finish the website design for a lawyer downtown and then start on Carla's stuff. I email Lucille and tell her Carla will be attending the open forum. Then I review her platform. I examine the platforms of the past four mayors and try to morph her focus points along the same track as those.

She's too heavy on the immigrant issue. Half of Key West is either Cuban, Haitian, or Eastern European. I try to focus on her desire for fiscal responsibility but her financial policy is too limiting. After working on it for a little while longer, I get frustrated and give up.

I head outside—the old couple is gone again—and work on the deck. Below me, the water laps at the shore, squeezing between browned mangrove roots. Stray chickens cluck at one another. It's finally feeling like winter, and I sit with a sweater curled around my shoulders until a car engine hums below.

I stand.

Footsteps on the stairs. I peer up from my spot on the deck and watch as Carla trudges up to the third floor. She wears jeans and a long-sleeved shirt, and her hair is wet. I can't see her face. I

40

place my laptop on my chair and make my way over to the stairwell. My stomach flutters. "This is a nice surprise," I say.

She cranes her neck, squinting in the early sunlight. A pair of extra-large, Army green colored sunglasses rests on her head. "Are you feeling better?" she asks.

"Did you come over just to see me?"

She fidgets, exhaling sharply. She looks like a child. "I think I left my phone here."

I climb the stairs. The wood planks of the stairs are cool against my bare feet. I'm still a little weak, probably from not eating. "You did?" I reach the top of the stairs, pressed into the landing space opposite her. The platform itself is only about three feet by three feet; we're close enough that I can smell her shampoo.

"Can I just check?"

"You seem nervous."

"I'm late," she says. Her eyes flicker away from mine. "Can you just let me in?"

I fight the smile that twitches my mouth. I think about how she looked in bed last night, small and delicate and mine.

I open the door and follow her in. The place still smells like lavender from the candle I burned last night, plus some lingering sweetness from the open container of orange juice. It feels like a million years ago that she was here, not merely a few hours. Carla bends over in front of me and looks beneath the couch. "There," she says.

I stare at her ass. "Oh, there it is."

She drops to her hands and knees, grunting. Her pants stretch tight. She reaches underneath the couch and drags her phone out. Then she rises, wiping her hands on her pants. Color fills her cheeks. She's faintly out of breath. "Do you want to go to the Rotary gala with me?" she asks. I stare at her, but she avoids my gaze. Sunlight streams in through the blinds, landing on the floor behind her. "I know you're already going. But I thought we could carpool."

"If you want to go on a date with me, Carla, just say so."

She rolls her eyes. "I think it's good for people to know you're working with me on the campaign. That's all."

A breeze flutters a stack of paperwork on the kitchen countertop. I feel a sudden unease, like the breeze could swoop in and pluck Carla away from me. I lean against the countertop and cross my arms over my chest. "Want me to pick you up?"

"That wouldn't make sense. You're closer to Key West."

"Let me," I say. "Think of it as making up for last night."

"You don't need to make up for that. I was worried."

"Carla, let me do this."

She shifts. She looks pudgy in the shirt she's wearing, but in a cute way that makes me want to fuck her senseless. Carla has always done that to me but now the feeling is so strong I can barely stand it.

TEN

Two weeks pass. Eli doesn't seem sick anymore and business picks up exactly as Carla thought it would. She officially lands the sale of a multi-million-dollar home on Duck Key. She gets three new referrals and picks up a client who runs half of the McDonald's franchise.

His information rests on the bedroom dresser in front of her as she sits, preparing for the gala. She's cleaned up her room but bottles of perfume and hair product still litter the nightstand and cabinet. She used half of them earlier in an attempt to reduce the volume of her hair for the Rotary gala this evening. The room smells like heat.

Carla places the curling iron back on the dresser and steps into her heels. She wears an older dress, a violet satin that clings to her shoulders and tapers off above her knees. Her hair looks better now that it's curled. She runs a hand over her stomach. It's flat enough but she's bigger than she's ever been. She can see it in her hips, her chest. Jeb would probably be on her about it, but he's been gone—a hunting competition in Texas. Yesterday, she told him to stay longer if he wanted. She doesn't need his help with the campaign, and it's not like he has to worry about working.

Outside her bedroom window, early night pours in. Her entire body is tense. Lately, all she can think about is the campaign, money, Eli. The thoughts run on repeat and no matter what she does, she can't get rid of them.

The tequila and tonic she poured herself earlier rests on the dresser, but she's afraid to drink it.

Eli will be here soon.

From the front of the house, the doorbell rings. She traces over her cleavage once before plucking up the tequila and club and downing it in three gulps. The alcohol goes straight to her belly, warming her and easing her tension. Screw it, she thinks. She's good at what she does. People know her and like her. There is no reason to be nervous.

Carla grabs her coat, and heads for the door to find Eli standing there. She looks good. Really good. She wears a black tux that's cut to fit her body and low-cut white top. A thin silver necklace with a tassel pendant rests along her breastbone. Her hair is pinned back on one side, hanging loose on the other. "Look at you," Carla says.

She's never seen it happen before, but Eli blushes. "You look really nice, too."

"I feel old."

Eli puts her hand on the dip of Carla's back. Her palm is warm. "You look hot. Ready?"

For a second, Carla just stands there, looking at Eli. Staring at her tux and necklace, the slimness of her collarbone. All of a sudden, she feels like she can't do this. It's wrong. They're friends. They work together.

"Carla?" Eli touches her wrist.

"I'm too old for proms," Carla says. "I don't know why I decided to do this."

The air around them is cool, but beads of sweat still form along her bra. Eli smirks. "You paid a hundred and fifty dollars for your ticket. Are you really going to waste that money?"

Carla hesitates.

What's the big deal? she tells herself. Calm down. They're just friends. Plus, she's already spent too much time fixing her hair. It would be a waste not to go out now.

• • •

The ride is quick and quiet. Eli talks the whole time. Instead of her normal, lackadaisical speech, her words are rapid and tight. She talks about a conflict with a client, then starts talking shit about the new Business Guild board member. Her knee bobs up and down as she drives.

They arrive at the gala, and Eli immediately gets them both drinks.

"Got you a tequila and tonic," she says, handing Carla a very large glass.

Carla hesitates, then brings the fizzing drink to her mouth. Bubbles burst against the bottom of her nose as she sips. "I shouldn't be drinking."

"Everyone is."

"I'm running for office."

"I know," Eli says. "Nobody in Key West trusts a dry politician."

For a few minutes, Carla leaves to chat with some other Rotarians before the program begins and when she comes back she finds Eli seated at a table in the back of the hotel ballroom, tucked into shadows. Eli doesn't say anything when she returns, just hands her another drink.

Carla sits. "You okay?"

"Fine," she says.

After the appetizers, the drinks really start to hit her. She's stopped listening to the speaker. His voice is just a low hum in the background. That's around that same time she notices Eli's hand on her knee. At first, it's just resting there, sending sparks up and down Carla's leg. But then it starts moving higher. Carla's belly starts to heat up. She's had too much to drink. Everything feels hot and fuzzy. She shifts, trying to get the throbbing between her legs to go away—tuning into the speaker, drinking water, smiling at their tablemates. But when Eli's hand slips just under the hem of her dress, Carla jumps in her seat. "You okay?" Eli asks.

Carla bites her lip, wanting to scream. "Fine."

She checks the program. They're only about halfway through.

She does everything she can to get comfortable but the throbbing between her legs is now unbearable. Heat crawls up her spine. She twitches as Eli's hand nestles high on her thigh, way too high. What is she doing? Playing games. Like she always does. Carla takes another sip of her tequila and turns.

Eli gazes calmly back.

And that's finally it—she can't take it anymore. It's the same way she felt in middle school being taunted by the older girls. One day she just snapped and hit one of them, socked the stupid bitch right in her chin.

She stands from her seat and Eli looks concerned. "Wait here," Carla says.

She leaves the ballroom and heads upstairs to the third floor of the hotel. It's quieter up here, even for a Saturday. A beige and maroon carpet leads her to the end of a long hallway where a private bathroom sits tucked in a corner. Sweat beads along her chest. Her hair feels heavy, weighted on her shoulders.

She's not gay. She's never even kissed another girl. It's just the intensity of everything. Eli plays games and plays them well. Everyone knows that.

She enters the bathroom and the lights flicker on. It's cool and quiet. Carla locks the door and leans forward against the tile wall. It's cool against her overheated skin. She closes her eyes and tries to think of something else, but all that's there is Eli and the campaign, Eli and the campaign.

There's nothing else she can do; she's got to get rid of the feeling.

After another minute, Carla hikes her dress over her hips and slips a hand between her legs.

ELEVEN

I've always been a drinker. Even back in middle school, I used to sneak Dad's whiskey from beneath the sink and mix it with Coca-Cola over ice. Sometimes I'd find half-ripe limes on the trees outside, and mix them in. Mimi never had a problem with my drinking. She said it would make me hearty and kill the bad things inside me.

At the gala, I drink tequila over ice after Carla abandons me to talk to more important people. I think maybe that will get rid of whatever negative energy is brewing in me, but it doesn't.

Being an adult in Key West is like being in high school again. There's a group of people who are in—the ones with money and clout—and the rest of us just go along as best we can. It's not what outsiders think. They see the palm trees, the turquoise water and loping banyans. But there is so much darkness in the Keys. Here, people use one another to climb the social food chain. They use their friends and neighbors like rungs, heels first, digging in hard.

At the podium, a microphone squawks and the presentation finally starts. Carla sits down next to me and I play with her knee, running my palm over her thigh, under the lip of her dress, delighting in the way her breathing picks up. Her skin grows warm under my touch but she doesn't move to stop me. She looks so flustered, all heat, her hair full of static but powerless to confront me, to hit me or yell at me like she would anywhere else. Seconds pass.

Abruptly, she pushes back her chair and stands to go to the bathroom. Her eyes are dark as she glares down at me. "Wait here."

My gut sparks. I shift, try to stand, but she puts her hand on my shoulder and she's strong. Heavy. I stay rooted in my chair, watching her as she turns and stalks out of the room.

The program continues at a snail's pace as I sit in the dark of the table, waiting on her. Our main courses arrive. Mine is duck—baked with a crispy skin on a bed of mashed potatoes. Green beans slick with oil spill steam on the side of the plate. Carla's main dish is steak. It's pink, bloody. Like she likes it.

She's been gone for several minutes now, long enough that I'm starting to get curious. I pick at my duck. At the front of the ballroom, some old white man is talking about a bunch of other dead white men.

Finally, Carla returns. Even in the dim light of the ballroom, I can see her skin is flushed and she's out of breath. Her dress sits crooked.

My body grows warm.

Carla sits. She reaches out for her napkin but I grab her wrist. She halts immediately, and her eyes go to mine. I can't help my-self—I bring her wrist to my mouth and kiss the skin there, just over the pulse point, and breathe in. Briefly, the scent of hand soap washes over me. I kiss her fingers and Carla blushes scarlet. Then I let her hand drop.

A feeling of satisfaction so deep and profound sweeps over my body. She has so much to learn about politics. And while she may be tough and she may be arrogant, she's not manipulative. Not enough. Campaigning down here is all about magic and tricks. Carla can't even hide the fact that she fucked herself in the bathroom.

"Should we leave?" I ask.

She stabs into her steak, mouth tight, eyes fuming. Blood leaks across the porcelain. "Eat your fucking food," she says.

• • •

Carla powers through two more tequila tonics before the end of the program. Then, the light on the stage softens and dance music starts to play. Some of the younger Rotarians go out—the fitness coach who I hate and her two sisters. They wear lace dresses, like small children, and their hair is so stiff it barely moves as they dance. I watch them for several minutes while Carla says goodbye to everyone. Then she grabs my hand and tugs me along behind her until we get to the car.

I'm not drunk, but I'm buzzed. She's drunk, though. Her eyes glaze and her mouth hangs in a frown that would make her un-attractive if not for the curve of her breasts in that dress and the way her eye makeup is done so stark. She looks mean.

"Are you okay?" I ask as we speed north on Route 1.

She puts a hand up to silence me and doesn't say another word the whole ride.

I test the *espiritus* and walk her to the front porch. Tension radiates off her but I'm calm, like I'm watching everything happen from outside of my body. I can see the scene—us in our dress clothes, the darkness around. The crickets are loud. Their noises spiral around me, thick as the heat, as Carla fumbles with her house keys in the dim light.

I take them from her hand and open the front door.

She hesitates and I think this is it, she's going to tell me to leave. She is always telling me to leave—in her eyes and her stature, the way she deflects personal questions, her voice growing tight. Yaurena did that to me, too. Before she left for California, she stopped talking to me altogether. I've never understood why, how. It's been over ten years and I still think of her when I eat paella or when I go to the Waterfront Playhouse. Part of me thinks she'll always be there.

• • •

Carla eventually invites me in.

We stand in the kitchen of her house. It smells like she's cleaned recently. The windows are open and a soft breeze moves over the couch. Carla has poured us both waters and they rest on the kitchen countertop, sweating rings in the dark green marble. I'm starting to feel different now. I'm more present. Heavy and raw.

"Did you have to be so sour all night?" she asks finally. "I should've brought Jeb."

"Fuck Jeb. He's a drunk."

"So are you."

In the light of the kitchen, Carla stares at me. But she doesn't look like she does at work. She looks withdrawn. Her gaze pulls back, away from me. An errant curl hangs in her face. "I treat you better than him," I say. Carla hesitates. Her dress is wrinkled near the armpits. I want to reach out and rip it off her. "You're scared."

"I'm not gay, Eli."

I drag my hand across the kitchen countertop and move in closer to her. "You still want to fuck me." Her breathing immediately goes shallow and it makes me crazy. I want to put my hand on her throat, squeeze and unsqueeze and watch how she gasps. A buzzing sensation starts in my stomach. It feels warm, like the first few shots of tequila. I move so I'm right up in her face, barely inches away. "You use him."

"I don't," she says. Her eyebrows knit tight. Her back is up against the countertop.

"I think you're just fucking him for his status." I lean in. I can smell the tequila on her breath. "Sell your pussy to get your name around town?"

The sting of her palm hits my cheek before I can register what's happening. She hits hard. Carla is not a slight woman by any means, and I can feel the strength of her in the hit. But I'm just as strong. And quicker. I grab her wrist as it retreats and slam it against the kitchen countertop.

She yelps, shifts. My cheek burns.

I think I could do really bad things to her now. I could hurt her. Scare her. Keeping one hand clenched around Carla's wrist, I place the other on her neck, tilting her chin so her throat is open, vulnerable. She makes a soft noise, almost like a whimper. Then I lean in and kiss her there, right over the pulse point. I think she might push me away, might tell me no but she doesn't.

She tilts her head back and exhales. Her skin is hot as the resistance in her body fades. I slip my knee between her legs and let go of her wrist to pull up the hem of her dress.

•••

I fuck her every way possible. With my mouth, with my hand, with the strap-on I shoved in my bag before leaving this afternoon. I have her on her back, on her hands and knees, bent over the bedroom dresser. Carla is a screamer and while I normally would worry about neighbors, I'm barely able to think about anything except for the feel of her skin, the wetness between her legs, and how I feel like I could devour her.

Near two am, her back is pressed up against the headboard of her bed, knees bent, the center of her spread to me. Faint light from the streetlamp filters in through the open bedroom window. It smells like damp night air, like sweat and salt. Carla's legs tremble. She's been on the brink of another orgasm for a while now, but I keep slowing down, stopping.

I pull back from her, watching her face contort.

"Eli—"

"What?"

She reaches her hand between her legs and I slap it away. There is so much darkness in me now, so deep even the sage couldn't burn it away. Her chest rises and falls, framed between her legs from my vantage point. Her stomach creases. For a girl with such curves, her belly is surprisingly flat. Carla grabs my hand and forces it between her legs. "Please."

I smirk up at her. Shadows rim her eyes. The hair around her face is matted with sweat. Her cheeks are damp. I have the momentary urge to push forward and kiss her, but I want more for her to hurt. I take her nipple in my mouth, pinch it between my teeth. She hisses, and when I pull away, she tries to force my mouth back between her legs. I pin her hands to the bed.

"Eli."

Sweat beads along her neck. She's thick there, almost manly looking if not for the large black curls that hang down over it. Like a husky football player. Her eyes are begging, like sapphire in the dim light. I want every part of her—her neck and scar, the faint stretch marks on her thighs.

I press back down to my stomach, forcing her legs as far apart as possible, and lay my mouth on her one more time.

TWELVE

Carla wakes up and her entire body is sore. Her thighs throb. Her head is dry and full of pressure. She rolls over in bed and finds a glass of water on the nightstand next to two salmon colored pills she assumes are Advil. She pops them in her mouth and chugs half the glass of water without stopping.

Light creeps into the room, warming the covers. She's alone. As the water rushes through her, she's able to sit up and look around. She wears an oversized Dolphins t-shirt and no underwear. Bruises line her thighs. She lifts up her shirt and hickies cover her left breast.

"Jesus Christ."

Carla rises and heads to the bathroom. She showers quickly and wraps a towel around her body, then heads to the kitchen, smelling coffee. She doesn't even care that Eli is the one handing it to her. She just takes the proffered cup and drinks. Droplets of water from her hair drip onto the floor. That's where she keeps her gaze—on the floor, away from Eli.

"I left," Eli says. "Then I decided to come back."

Carla drinks. The central air comes on, springing goosebumps across her skin. The coolness feels good on her aching muscles. "Why?"

"Because we need to talk."

Carla hesitates. Part of her is too hungover to care about this—she's fucked her fair share of douchey guys in bars before Miles was born. Part of her says she was fine after those, so she'll be fine after this. Part of her says this is different. This won't be fine. "I can't talk now."

"I'll make breakfast."

"You can't cook."

"Of course I can," Eli snaps.

Carla lifts her gaze. Eli wears a muscle tee and jeans, her hair down. Damp. She's got on a pair of thick black glasses and underneath them her eyes are dark. She looks good, as always. Carla is so fucking sick of how good this girl always looks. "I'm not your girlfriend, Eli."

Eli hesitates, then smirks. "I penetrated pretty much every opening in your body last night. It warrants a conversation."

Warmth floods Carla's body. She feels it in her cheeks first, then in her stomach, then where the bruises are. She hates this—hates talking, hates being naked in the light, hates that she doesn't want Eli to go. She swallows and places the coffee mug on the table. "I'm going to get dressed. You can make breakfast if you want."

• • •

In the bedroom, she can't stop touching the marks on her body. She stands in front of the closet mirror for close to five minutes, just feeling her skin—the dimples and stretch marks, the tender spots and bruises.

She's firmed up a lot since last year, even though she's put weight on. Isn't walking supposed to take the weight off? She touches her stomach, her thighs. Eli made a huge deal over her thighs. She's never been with someone who's spent so much time on her thighs and breasts before. Usually it's just bam, bam, bam, done. Sometimes Jeb can be good, but only when he feels like putting in the time, which isn't often.

Carla finds a pair of black sweatpants and pulls them on, along with an oversized t-shirt. It chafes sliding over her breasts and she hisses.

This can't happen again. It's inappropriate. She's seventeen years older than Eli. They have nothing in common. Eli is one of those girls who think bathrooms should be shared and men should wear rompers and skirts if they want. She has no idea what this world is really like.

THIRTEEN

I've never been a very good hostess, but I can cook breakfast like nobody's business. When Dad was amid his cancer treatment, the only thing that could settle his stomach was my breakfasts—potatoes dusted in paprika and bacon bites.

There's no grease in the house, so I fry the bacon strips in butter and a small amount of water. By the time Carla returns, dressed now, the smell of the food fills the room, along with the sound of sizzling butter. Carla's in sweatpants and a t-shirt, her hair down and softly styled. It makes my breath catch in my chest. I look down at the skillet and pick off several strips of bacon, placing them on a paper towel on the countertop. It soaks up the oil quickly.

Carla snatches one up and drops it immediately.

"It's hot," I say. As she shifts next to me, I catch a whiff of her perfume. She shifts, blows softly on the cooling strips, then brings a piece to her mouth again. A sound of pleasure escapes her. "Good?"

"So good."

The next few strips sizzle as I lay them down. A batch of diced potatoes cooks in the oven and the smell of them inundates—paprika and cheese dust that I found for microwave popcorn. Oven heat warms my leg. Carla lingers, muscles tense. I'm tense, too. Heavy somehow. I couldn't sleep at all. Carla fell asleep around 3:30 in the morning and I lay awake after that, just watching, tracing circles on the tips of her breasts. She slept soundly. "This is really good, Eli."

"I used to make it for my dad when he was sick."

Carla's quiet for a moment. Then, "I forgot he had cancer. Do you still talk with him?"

I shrug. "Every couple of months or so."

Smoke rises. The ceiling fan hums. I turn off the skillet and oven, grab an oven mitt and pull out the tray of potatoes. They're perfect—nice and browned but still soft on the inside, coated in a fine layer of paprika and popcorn cheese dust. Oil bubbles on their skins. I sprinkle pepper over them and remove a fork from the drying rack.

Carla snatches it from my hand and stabs at a piece.

She chews. "This can't happen again."

"What, breakfast?"

"You know what I mean."

She chews. Easy like nothing's wrong. Like nothing's at stake. "It won't," I say.

She stabs at another potato. She holds the fork funny, like a kid. Not between her thumb and index finger but in a fist. It fits her in some way. She's always stabbing through life, hacking away at things. "I didn't know you could do this."

I turn to look at her. She's perfect in the early light—unmade, bags under her eyes, her hair limp and wet on her shoulders. I love her so much in this moment, I feel like I could die. "There's a lot you don't know about me."

"Like what?"

"I used to study circus when I was a kid," I say. Carla stares at me, a slight smirk on her lips. "I'm very flexible." The smirk immediately disappears. I grab a piece of bacon and shove it in my mouth. It burns. I chew the hell out of it and swallow as quickly as possible while Carla pours herself another cup of coffee. "It's going to be okay," I say.

"Of course it will be." She brings the coffee to her lips and steam obscures her face. It seems like she doesn't care at all. Like last night was just another night to her when I feel like I'm crawling out of my skin, like I'll die if she sends me away, even though I know she will.

•••

Predictably, she does send me away. She sits down at the kitchen table after eating and sifts through the newspaper with her back to me. I clean the kitchen and leave without saying another word. I fume on the drive south, and have to force myself to take deep breaths. I watch the sunlight cluster behind the clouds and tell myself that I live in paradise. There's good pussy everywhere. If not Carla, then someone else.

I roll the windows down and let the breeze in. The air smells clean today, absent that thick salt and sea stink that hangs on the roots of the mangroves. I'm exhausted but wired. Pressure pushes in around my temples.

As soon as I arrive at the house, my phone rings.

"Hey Mimi."

"Are you okay?"

I unbuckle and gather my purse. "Why? Was there a disturbance in The Force?"

"What is The Force? I asked if you were okay."

A breeze sweeps up off the sea, bathing my body in salt water. I exhale. "Not really."

"What has happened?"

I climb the stairs to the apartment. The pit of my stomach is upset and I wonder if I'm going to be shitting my pants for the next week until something gives. "Nothing," I say. "I just don't feel good."

Mimi is silent on the other line like she has been a million times before. We used to joke in high school that she didn't need to live here in the Keys with me, she could feel everything that was going on just by my voice and the pattern of my speech through the phone. "Why do you lie? Do you think I can't tell?"

"Mimi, I just don't feel like talking about it." I unlock the apartment and the smell of old sage wafts out. I can't believe that the stink is still here. Usually it dissipates after a day or two. I drop my purse on the table and open the living room windows, clenching the phone between my ear and shoulder. "It's a woman," I finally

57

admit. "I don't know what to do. I really like her."

"And does she like you?"

I head to the fridge and pop open a beer. "Well, she slept with me so..."

Mimi sighs. "I sense something heavy in you, pet."

I hop up onto the kitchen countertop and bring the beer to my mouth. The liquid fizzes as it slides down my throat, burning warmly in my stomach. "What does that even mean?"

"You know what it means."

A prickling sensation lingers on my neck. I put the beer down. Tiredness lingers behind my eyes. I feel hollow and achy and before I can stop them, tears spring to my eyes. I don't know why it's so wrong. Why I can't want someone just for myself after all these years of sitting in luncheons alone and going to dinner alone and watching the sun spirals in the morning in an empty apartment. "Yeah," I say.

"Tell me."

My throat is tight. "It didn't even mean anything."

"Did you read it in a book?"

"No. I just did what felt right." It's almost like I can hear her face changing—her eyes welling, the practiced calm that takes over her muscles. I wish I were more like her but I'm not. I can't shove my feelings down and pretend they're not there. "I love her."

"You might but you can't do that."

"I didn't do anything." Mimi is quiet again and I remember how I felt when Yaurena left. How sick I was. I tried everything I could to get her back but after a while she stopped texting me back, stopped calling. The worst part wasn't her leaving, but the feeling afterwards of realizing it was finally over. "Mimi, I have to go."

"You shouldn't see her anymore. Okay, pet? I love you and I want you to be healthy."

"I gotta go," I say. I feel heavy in a way I haven't before. "I love you, too."

FOURTEEN

A large part of Carla hates the socializing that comes with running for office, but something else in her enjoys it. Over the next two weeks, she gets invited to six parties and private happy hours. One afternoon, she's asked to host a party at Looe Key Tiki Bar. Another night, Mangrove Mama's holds a happy hour benefit for her.

Her business booms; she closes two deals, gains three new clients—all exceptionally wealthy.

The only problem is that she's not sleeping well. She wakes up at two in the morning most nights and can't get back to sleep. She limits communication with Eli to only email. It helps a little, but not really. She wakes up at night and paces. She drinks tea. She goes for walks along the avenue. Time passes but nothing changes. Sometimes deep in the height of the night, she thinks of Eli and her hand slips between her legs. This is what she hates most. It happens over and over.

Then, it's time for the first open political forum.

•••

In high school, Carla used to vomit before every class presentation she had to make. It didn't help that she wore ugly dresses and didn't have any friends. Like clockwork, five minutes before every science presentation, every English presentation, she'd run like hell to the high school bathroom and barf her brains out into a green toilet bowl.

She has the same feeling now, seated behind a long skinny table in the board room of the Marathon board of county commissioners building. Four other candidates sit at the table with her, each with microphones placed in front of them. The room is full, but no Jeb. She hasn't talked to him in weeks.

It's six pm on a Wednesday and she expected less people.

A tightening sensation tugs on her gut. Her eyes sting but she won't cry. Carla stopped crying back in '98 when her husband left her with an infant. There was no time for crying then. Miles did enough of it for her.

She straightens her pants—black today. The only ones she doesn't feel fat in.

"You ready?"

She looks up to find Eli standing over her. A feeling she can't describe crashes over her body. She feels warm and at the same time, calm. Like being in the water at the beach. Her eyes sting again. She blinks the tears away and stands up.

FIFTEEN

"What?" I ask. "Did you think I wouldn't show up?"

Carla looks like she's a second away from barfing her brains out. Her cheeks are pale and her eyes lack their normal sparkle. She's dressed neatly but it looks like she's prepared for a funeral, not an open forum with her black trousers and a black blouse. Barely an inch of her skin shows. She teeters on black heels. "We can't talk here," she says. "The mics."

Her pants tighten around her ass as she leads me to the side of the stage, climbing down a set of stairs away from the microphones and lights. It's quieter here, but I can still feel the hum of the room. There are so many people. "You're nervous," I say.

"I'm fine, Eli."

"You reviewed the talking points I gave you?"

Beads of sweat pebble on her upper lip. I reach out and place my hand on her neck, just below her scar. Her skin burns and her pulse is light and rapid. I let my hand drop as a local photographer sidles up behind her. "Can I grab you two for a photo?" he asks.

"No," I say. "We're busy."

"It'll just take a second."

"I said not right now."

He stares at me a moment, then looks down at Carla. She offers him a smile but it falls so flat, I almost laugh. "Okay," he says. "Thanks." He lowers his camera and walks away, and when I breathe in, I can taste his cologne, cheap and chemical.

"Did you have to be rude to him?" Carla snaps.

"Did you review the talking points?"

She glares at me, then reaches into her trouser pocket to pull out several lined index cards. They're bent, scuffed around the edges like she's been playing with them. "I even wrote them all down. See?"

"Good. Then you'll be fine."

"I know that," she says sharply, but then her lips pinch together, springing worry lines around her mouth. This is the part of her that's always gotten to me the most, the way she hesitates but at the same time lashes out. The way she boulders forward, then checks behind her to make sure she hasn't hurt anyone. There's so much of her that's contrary, like she's fighting over every single decision she makes.

"People like you, Carla. Just stick to your points, okay?"

She's quiet. It's just the sound of the room—the low buzz of the mics and the audience murmuring. The stink of the old carpeting balloons around me. I wonder if things would feel different if we were outside. If the soft sway of the palms and the smell of the plumeria blooms would ease her tension.

But I like this room with its bad electrical connections and carpet that needs to be replaced. This is the real Key West. Dig down under the palms, Spanish limes, and poincianas, the drunken parades on Duval, six toed cats and blue feathered roosters—it's all just rot at the core.

•••

Watching Carla speak is just about the funniest thing I've ever seen. I can tell by her eyes and the way she holds herself that she's crawling out of her skin. Her shoulders are forward instead of back and she squints, like she's fearful of the audience. Still, she does well with the talking points and speaks low and smooth. Her voice is what saves her.

"ICE agents have just deported a Russian immigrant living in Key West," the moderator says. "What are your thoughts on that, Carla?"

She sucks in a breath. Smiles. If not for my cards, she would tell the moderator to take all the immigrants away. Including me. This is America, she'd say. But with my direction, she pauses before leaning into the mic. "That concerns me," she says. "This man has no criminal record. He works and pays taxes."

Just like I've told her, she stops. After a pause, the moderator thanks her, then asks another candidate the same question.

I let go of the breath I was holding.

After the forum is over, she shakes hands, working the room like she's supposed to. She talks to the business guild president, some journalists. No one of real importance. When she's done, she makes her way over to me. She seems dangerous all of a sudden, this mass of nerves and fire, stalking forward on those heels, which she never wears. She looks like she needs to be fucked. Hard.

"Did I do okay? I didn't sound stupid?"

I stare down at her. She's red in her cheeks. Her freckles stand prominent. "You did great," I say. "You didn't get off topic once."

"It was fine, though? You're sure?"

I stay quiet, just staring down at her until the tension lines between her eyebrows fade and she forces a smile.

"Do you want to go to dinner?" she asks.

Tightness weaves through my chest. I turn away from her, looking out into the room. I'm not sure what I'm searching for—a distraction maybe, something to remind me of what a god-awful pain in the ass Carla can be. But there's nothing. No one else holds my attention anymore. I look back at her. "Let's get pizza to go." I'm pleased with how calm I sound. "We'll eat at your place."

The room is rapidly emptying now. The moderator is gone, and only one other candidate is still here, the local photographer snapping pictures of him as he greets the last remaining audience members.

I touch her arm. "Carla?"

"Okay," she says. "I'll meet you there."

• • •

It's grown much hotter since I first started working on Carla's campaign. Now deep in April, the air holds a humidity that was absent at the start. It hangs around me as I sit on the porch, waiting for her. The only sound is the water out back lapping at the dock.

Soon her car lights illuminate the darkness.

I stand. On the drive over here, I drank a rum and coke out of a Yeti cup. The buzz burns its way through me as Carla plods up the steps. "I thought you were getting pizza," she says.

"It's coming."

She eyes me, then fumbles with her keys. "You smell like alcohol."

"So what? I'm not working."

She manages to unlock the door and steps in, immediately taking off her heels. I can see the imprints of her feet in them.

"Are you okay?" I ask.

She pads across the floor. The house is shadowed by dim light from the moon and stinks of cleaning detergent.

"Carla?"

"I need a tequila," she says. "Let me drink."

She goes straight for the fridge and pours herself a glass of tequila on the rocks. She drinks deeply, grimaces, then her eyes flicker up to mine. Blue flecked with amber. I pass around her and pour my own glass. "You did well. And you looked good. But I told you to wear green."

"The green shirt makes me look fat." She brings the tequila to her lips again, then sets the glass on the counter. A piece of her hair is caught behind her ear, poking out errantly. She looks messy, goofy. I let it linger there.

"What gives?" I ask. "You run away from me for two weeks and now we're having a pizza date?"

Carla shifts. She grabs the glass of tequila again. I've never seen her drink this quickly before. Her lips grow wet with it, her cheeks pink. She looks her age. "I wanted to see you."

I wait but she doesn't say more. That's when the doorbell rings—the pizza. I don't look away at first; I need this moment, I need her to tell me she needs me, she can't do this without me, but then she turns her head and says, "I'll get it."

She tries to brush past me but I grab her by the arm and push her back so she knocks against the refrigerator. For a second, she looks surprised—her eyes widen and her mouth opens but she doesn't say anything. I think of how she looked the morning after we slept together, that haughtiness in her eyes, like somehow she had gained the upper hand. For two weeks, she didn't take my calls. She'd only email, and it was just about the campaign.

A muscle in my neck tightens. I let go, laughing at her shock.

This is nothing, I want to say. You have no idea. This is barely a fraction of what those two weeks felt like. This is what you get for turning me away.

•••

I go to the front door and pay the delivery man myself, hefting the steaming hot pizza box from his hands and shutting the door behind me with my foot. I lay the pizza on the kitchen table as Carla sets down some plates. They're the cheap kind, white Nantucket. I recognize them because they're what Dad gave me when I left for college. "I would've paid."

"You're a shitty tipper."

She makes a sound of protest, then falls silent.

"What's with you?" I ask.

Carla's hand lingers on the napkins between the plates. Then she looks up at me. It's clear the tequila has already taken effect—her beautiful blue eyes carry a glaze. "I get nervous when I have to speak in front of crowds."

I open the pizza box. The smell of grease plumes. Half of the pizza is covered in mushroom and sausage—Carla's half. My half is moons and half-moons of pepperoni, pocketed with puddles of oil. "I don't believe that. I've seen you give presentations to a dozen buyers."

"That's work."

"This is too, now," I say. I plop a piece of pizza on my plate and do the same to hers. She just stares at it. Steam rises. I wipe my hand on a napkin and set it down on the table, watching her face carefully. She looks pathetic, like she might cry. All of a sudden, all the anger, the spite inside me falls away. "Hey." I move closer. She doesn't pull away; I wrap my arms around her and bring her into me. "You did great. Stop worrying."

She exhales, and I can feel her breath on my skin. It gives me goosebumps. She shifts, then settles in my arms. Her hair brushes my chin. Her fingers grip my shirt and I feel like an asshole for wanting her right now, but I do. Her hands rest on my lower back, palms warm. We stay like that for a while until some of the tension leaves her body. Then I pull back. I run my hand down her arm, tracing around the freckles and sun spots. "I'm fine," she says.

"You're always fine."

She makes a face. "I don't know if this is such a good idea."

I still. The ceiling fan spins above us. All I can smell is the grease, the meat. I feel like a douchebag because she's upset, and I really want to stay mad at her. But I can't. "If what's a good idea?"

"This whole campaign."

I smile. My hands linger; kneading the muscles in her shoulders. She's freakishly tense there—lined with muscle, the kind that's heavy but not visible. "Since when I have you ever backed down from a challenge?"

Carla smiles but she feels different now. It's like some fairy dust has settled over her, softening her to me. At the same time, I feel like I'm being pilled tighter, closer to her than ever.

SIXTEEN

She's starting to feel a little better, and the pizza helps. Eli eats three slices. Carla wants to eat three slices, but only manages to get through one and a half. Then she picks off two of Eli's pepperonis and watches the younger woman's face morph.

"If you wanted pepperoni, you should've told me," Eli says. She gathers both of their plates and heads for the sink.

"I didn't know I wanted them until I saw them."

Carla stands. She feels stronger now—maybe the whole thing was just low blood sugar. She gathers the dirty napkins but before she can do anything else, Eli's at her side again. "I'll take care of this."

A shiver races through her body. Carla exhales. The table is clear in a matter of seconds, except for their drinks. She shouldn't be drinking so much, especially not around Eli, but she almost can't help it. Sometimes these days she wakes up and feels like her body moves forward all on its own, like she's being pulled by a string. "I'm going to shower." She's suddenly exhausted, but not in a bad way. "You can stay tonight."

Eli turns to look at her from the sink. "Is that a request or a demand?"

Warmth floods Carla's belly. She touches her stomach, then lets her hand fall again. "I can't make you do anything."

A funny look takes over Eli's face. She looks down at the floor, then turns back to the dishes. The sink sprays mist into the air as she scrubs.

Carla heads for the bathroom.

After the forum was over, a ringing started in her ears and didn't stop until she got home. She could hear but was distracted by the sound. All those people who talked to her afterwards... she had no idea what half of them they were saying.

In the bathroom, Carla strips of her clothes. She folds her pants and puts them on the ledge of the bathroom sink, then starts the shower. Hot water sprays across the tile. She ties her hair up and steps in.

After the ringing sound stopped, this sense of relief swept over her. It was similar to how she felt after seeing her ex-husband in court for the first time during their divorce. After it was over, she felt powerful for having done it, no matter how much she dreaded it beforehand.

Carla lathers soap over her chest and stomach. The smell of vanilla and spice rises with the heat. She pictures Eli standing in the kitchen, washing dishes and cleaning. She's never seen Eli be domestic before. Never thought of her in that way. Eli is good for two things—working with technology and pissing people off.

She rinses the suds from her body and towels off. The lights are off in the apartment except the hallway and when she enters the bedroom, she finds Eli under the covers already, her nose in a detective book with the night stand lamp on. She feels shy as she peels the towel off and slips into a t-shirt and shorts. "Where did you find that?" she asks.

Eli doesn't look at her. "On the dresser. Under a pile." Carla slips under the covers. "It's shit."

She shifts, lays her head so she's on her side, facing Eli. Now that the buzz from the tequila has worn off, her mind starts working again. She's not sure exactly why she's letting this happen. She is not gay. Eli is too young. There are a million things wrong with the situation.

Eli turns, meets her gaze, and as if reading her mind says, "Sleep, Carla. It's okay."

Warmth floods her body again. There's got to be something good about this, she decides. People are noticing her. Things are changing, she can feel it. And she's learned things. Facebook.

Press release writing. With Eli, she doesn't feel so stupid asking questions.

Carla glances over Eli's resting form—the muscles in her arms. The tattoos. It doesn't feel bad to be here like this. It doesn't feel wrong and no one is ever going to know.

Carla rolls on her back so she can breathe better and closes her eyes. It takes a long time to fall asleep but when she does, she sleeps better than she has in a month.

SEVENTEEN

The next afternoon when I finish work, I stab Route 1 with Carla's signs all the way from Big Coppitt down to the triangle. They've turned out well. She's a thousand times prettier than the other mayoral candidates and the look in her picture makes her seem capable. Not that she isn't inherently capable, but I have doubts. Carla isn't as hard as some of the candidates. She lacks the kill switch they all seem to have.

I grab a six pack at the Big Coppitt Shell and the owner asks me to put one of her signs out on the strip of grass in front of the gas pumps. This has happened to me before, once on Summerland when I was driving up to meet a client and another time on Big Pine when I was going to a Lower Keys Rotary meeting.

After placing the last sign out by the road at the station, I head back to Carla's house.

She's just finished making dinner when I arrive—homemade Conch chowder. She hasn't asked me to come over but there are two bowls out, two napkins. The Conch chowder is a hell of a lot better than her meatloaf. It's full of meat and potatoes and is spicy but not too spicy. We eat at the kitchen table in front of my laptop, reviewing her voter pools. I sop up the soup broth with a loaf of focaccia. An open beer rests in front of me.

"Everyone I've talked to said you did well last night." I shove more bread in my mouth, swallow. "You were firm. Not a blabbermouth. You do, though," I take a sip of beer, "need to work on your demeanor."

"My demeanor?"

I put my bread down on a napkin. I'm faintly aware of how I smell like beer and she smells like cilantro from the soup. "You seemed kind of aloof is what some viewers said."

"I was nervous."

"Next time, pretend you're excited."

She purses her lips and plays with her spoon, mixing it around her almost-empty bowl with a thoughtless irritation that I love. I thought about her all day at work almost non-stop. And while part of me knows this isn't healthy, another part of me doesn't care.

Carla puts her spoon down. She reaches out and grabs my beer, bringing it to her lips. "I want to win," she says.

I stare down at her. "I thought you weren't sure about this whole thing?"

She's quiet, looking at the kitchen table. There's a gleam in her eye. I've seen her get it sometimes when she's at Rotary or when she's working a deal with a buyer. She has this competitiveness in her that comes out every once in a while—it's like a spell that takes over. We played trivia once at a happy hour function and she got so into it I was embarrassed for her. "I like most of it," she says. "Just not some things."

"You like the attention."

"I'm a good candidate."

"You are," I say. "I'm proud of what you've done so far."

I finish the beer and close up the laptop. It's nearing ten o'clock and I should go, but I'm not going to. My overnight bag rests on the kitchen countertop. The apartment has been tidied. Her papers have been forced off into corners. Outside, the moonlight is so strong, I can see the palm fronds waving in the window.

Carla rises, placing her dishes in the sink and running water over them. She takes mine and does the same. She's in stretchy black pants, like yoga pants, a pair I've never seen her in before. She looks strangely domestic with her hair all curly and wild and no make-up, standing over the sink with the light shining pale on her skin. "I'm going to bed," she says. "Are you coming?"

I idle. My beer is gone but I hold the bottle in front of me. "It's a little early for sleep."

She turns. Her eyes flicker. "Who says I'm going to sleep?"

The corners of my mouth twitch. I place my beer on the counter and grab her hand, pulling her along behind me as I make my way to her bedroom. For once in my life, I feel calm. Like I belong somewhere. There's no pressure in my stomach. I want to tell her this, but I also sense something temporary, and it keeps me quiet.

•••

That night, it's different. She doesn't scream. She whimpers and sighs. Her breath trails out like the hush of the wind. I take my time with her. She feels changed, but so much the same, like getting down to the core of her, she's all questions and softness and vulnerability.

Afterwards, she turns to me and says, "You think I'm a pillow princess."

I'm on my back, looking up at the ceiling, out of breath. My muscles protest, tired. My lips are wet with her still. "Where did you learn that term?"

"On the internet."

I turn to look at her; her hair is curly and mussed. Her lips look burned by pink Chapstick, her wrinkles prominent in the light. I love the curve of her breast, the slope and slight slack from having been pregnant. She is organic in a way that makes me want to tuck her away inside myself and keep her there forever. "So, prove you're not."

She blinks feather light eyelashes. Rolls on her side so she's staring up at me and her palm goes to my belly. I immediately still. My skin pulls tight with goosebumps. She kisses me and her hand moves lower. It curves over my hipbone, over my thigh. Then she's inside me and I can't do anything but focus on breathing. Her hair spirals over me.

How things change. In less than two months. Everything is different now.

...

We fall into a pattern.

I work on my own projects during the day. They've grown numerous. Most evenings, I pack a bag and head for Carla's. She never tells me to go, and whenever I show up, there's always enough food on the table for two. A few times, I find Fat Tire, my favorite beer restocked in the fridge.

Mimi calls twice in this time period but I don't call her back. The summer hits heavy— the skies bleed red and pink every morning with the rising sun. It rains most days, usually in the afternoon and afterwards the rain lingers in the air like a wet blanket hanging over everything. The poincianas explode with color. The firemen's association endorses Carla, then the sheriff's department. Her face starts to take on a winner's glow, even though the election isn't until November.

...

In early June, Carla is invited to a fundraiser at Blue Heaven downtown in Bahama Village. The temperature is in the mid-eighties, cooler than it has been. Carla's in rare form— on two hours of sleep after making a huge sale the day before and wearing a tapered khaki skirt. A trail of sweat dampens the spine of her sleeveless blouse by the time we reach the restaurant.

A rooster squawks as we enter. Blue Heaven is open-air, hidden under palms and Christmas tree lights. The bar is full and a live band plays Smokey Robinson behind it. I keep my hand on Carla's lower back where moisture beads through her shirt.

"Drink?" I ask.

She looks up at me. She's so tired her eyes are glazed over, even though I know she hasn't touched a drink yet. "I can't."

I get her a tequila and tonic anyway and we sit down in the corner. A waiter walks around with mini cheeseburgers and I take two, shoving the first in my mouth before noticing Carla isn't eating anything. I swallow once, then ask, "What's up?"

She looks around the space. The current city mayor is here, along with a group from the Studios of Key West. A couple of other semi-familiar faces pass by but no one especially interesting. No one we really need to win over. Carla puts her drink down on the table. "I don't want to be here."

"Then why'd we come?" I ask. Her gaze turns to a glare. She looks out at the band again, the vein in her forehead straining. I've seen her like this before—once at happy hour right before she had to leave because she was having a panic attack. "Let's leave. You've been to enough of these."

She turns back to me. "You think?"

"Come on."

I place my half-eaten second cheeseburger on the table. Gulp back the rest of my beer. I'm hungry but not starving. Lately, part of me has felt full in a way I haven't in years. I hold my hand out to Carla. She looks at me but doesn't take it. "Eli..."

"Let's get grilled cheese," I say.

She stares at me for several seconds before tilting her head slightly. Then she stands. I think in this moment, this is the best things are ever going to get. A woman I love came to this party with me. She's going to leave with me. She's going to sit in the car while I drive us home and press her lips against mine before I fall asleep.

•••

It's a short walk to Mary Ellen's restaurant. The bar is dim and empty. Music plays through speakers but it's not nearly as loud as it was before. I order Carla a margarita from the tap and a grilled cheese with cold cuts. I get an IPA and the Thomas—grilled cheese with bacon and blue cheese. We sit at the bar, next to each other, facing forward. The heat of her body warms mine as she takes a deep bite and sighs. A piece of meat slips from between

75

the bread as she chews, falling to the plate. She takes it between her fingers, then brings it to her mouth.

"Mom taught me to make grilled cheese," she says.

I chew. "Yeah?"

"I burned my hand on the stove once." She busies herself with the melted cheese, twisting it around the edges of the bread, licking it off her fingers. "Didn't go to the doctor's."

"Why?"

"We lived in rural New York. There weren't any close by."

I take her hand in my own and examine it. No burn scars, just freckles, a thin band of emeralds on her middle finger and a white streaked scar across her knuckle. I bring my hand to my mouth and kiss the scar. There's no one watching. No one cares. It's perfect and quiet, just the two of us in our own world.

EIGHTEEN

The summer heat becomes unbearable. Carla can't go outside for more than five minutes before getting sick and angry with it. The newscasters say it's the hottest summer in Key West history. Salt winds blow in from Cuba. Besides the heat, she feels strangely calm. Miles has chosen to stay in Gainesville for the summer to take classes and she's glad in a way to have him away from all this. In the evenings, she watches Eli tilt back beers and work on the computer. She can do things in seconds that would take her months—make websites and posters and things. Carla sits for hours, just watching her.

One night, Carla dreams she's at the BottleCap in downtown Key West. One of the county commissioners is on her left and the head of the firemen's association is on her right. The room is blurred at the edges, like maybe she's been drinking too much. Everyone watches the television. She keeps looking around for Eli but Eli isn't there. Then the county commissioner leans over and whispers in her ear, "Stop looking for your dyke bitch, Carla. She isn't here."

Carla wakes up with a start. Her ear tickles, like someone's been whispering in it. The light is on in the bedroom and when she turns, she finds Eli snuggled up with a large book in the spot next to her. She reaches out immediately and grabs her wrist. "Eli."

"What?"

Carla's grip tightens. She feels strangely weak. "I had a dream I won. But you weren't there."

Eli lays the book flat on her chest. "Of course I'll be there," she says, but Carla keeps holding on. Eli's pulse beats, sure and strong beneath her skin. "Carla?"

It's only ten thirty but it feels like she's been asleep for hours. Carla sits up in bed and grabs the water on the nightstand. She drinks deep, then rubs her face. She doesn't like this feeling. It's the same she got when Miles was a baby. Always worrying, always waiting for the other shoe to drop. Like something this good and precious couldn't really belong to her.

Carla leans forward. Soon after, Eli's arms are around her waist. Warmth. Eli kisses her neck. Her muscles relax and she tilts. More warmth. "Eli..."

"What?"

Carla finds Eli's hand and brings it to her chest. Sadness sweeps over her. She doesn't want to feel this way. She doesn't want to have drama. She just wants things to be easy for once in her life.

She holds still. Quiet. The fan spins. Eli leans in and kisses her again, her hand moving to Carla's breast. Her mouth tastes like tea. Bergamot. Carla lays back on the bed, letting the pillow cushion her neck. How many times have they done this now? Not enough to make her want it any less. She shouldn't want it at all.

Still, heat floods her belly as Eli shifts on top of her. Carla bends her knees, cradling Eli between her thighs. Then a hand is in her hair, and Carla closes her eyes, just feeling.

NINETEEN

On July 1st, I take Carla to a gala in Marathon held by a local interior design company to aid the firemen's house. It's the hottest day it's been so far—ninety degrees with seventy percent humidity. There's barely a breeze.

Although Carla sometimes sells real estate up there, I'm hardly ever up this way and don't know anyone in the room. And while most of the time I hate being in a room with a bunch of other people, I'm well-known in Key West and people stay away from me. Here, it's different. This crowd skims right over me like I don't even exist.

Carla seems fine. She wears a dress again, a green one that she bought just for this. I'm in white pants and a black blouse, a tight white jacket. Carla's hair is curled. She smells like salon shampoo and her freckles stand prominent on her recently tanned skin. She wears diamond earrings. I bought them for her three days ago.

The gala is inside and the showroom lights are down low, the air on high. Goosebumps line my spine. I want to put my hand on Carla as we pass through the couples but I don't know these people. They're older than the crowd I know in Key West, and many are men. They wear oversized black tuxes, and most of them are at least seventy years old. The room smells. Something like old people and money and air that's been swallowed too many times.

Carla talks to almost every single person.

I trail behind her with a glass of tequila in my hand. I feel stupid. Useless. I can't find our seats and when I finally do, they're labeled, "Carla Hansen," and "Carla Hansen guest."

"Oh good," I tell her. "I'm so glad they know who I am."

But Carla isn't paying attention to me. Her gaze is turned, set on a sixty-something man in a nice suit. He has disheveled hair but an irritated look on his face that makes him seem important. After Carla addresses him, I realize he's the mayor of Marathon.

He shakes her hand and tells her he's voting for her in November. Her face lights up like nothing I've seen before. Her smile is huge. I can't help thinking that nothing I do has ever made her look like that.

I sit down at the table and take a pull of tequila.

•••

After the programming starts, it's not too bad. The chicken is good and I drink hard on the open bar. But there's something wrong about tonight. The heat from outside floods through the walls. I take my suit jacket off and trail it over the back of my chair. I rest my arm on the back of Carla's chair. At first, I think she's going to tell me to move but she just leans back against it, then quickly pats my thigh.

I relax a little, but not completely.

The last time I felt like this in a room of people was back in high school. I was seventeen, a senior and gearing up for a graphic design degree at the University of Virginia. The Key West Noon Rotary decided to give me a small scholarship. Dad was gone by then—he was living in an apartment in Tavernier to run the resort at Amara Cay, so I attended the presentation alone. They harped on my immigrant status, my work in the LGBT student group. But I knew they picked me because although I was an immigrant, I was white, and although I was vocal in the LGBT student group, I wasn't butch. I sat there feeling stupid. No one asked me how I was. No one chatted with me. I sat and ate my pie, listened to the speaker, and smiled for the camera when I was told.

A waiter places a slice of chocolate cake in front of me. I edge the frosting, dragging it across the soft part of the cake.

I finish the slice; Carla does not.

By that point, I've had three glasses of tequila and am working on my fourth. The presentation part of the night ends and then everyone starts to get up and talk. I just sit there, watching. I keep my arm on Carla's chair even after she's risen to speak with people again. After a while, I start to feel eyes on me. I look up.

About ten feet away from the table, the owner of a major hotel chain in the Keys, Jim, stands with his wife and Carla, chatting. They face me; Carla's back is to me. Although the commissioner isn't looking at me, his wife is. Her mouth is tight, in a line. They're younger than most of the rest of the people here, probably a little above Carla's age. His wife stares. I stand. Her eyes stay focused on me as I walk over.

"Hi," I say. "I don't think we've met. I'm Eli."

I offer my hand but no one takes it. Jim smiles, but it's close-mouthed, like a teacher would give a small child who's just thrown a tantrum. I can smell his old man cologne. He's balding, and the bald spot sweats lightly. "Eliza, isn't it? I met your father once."

"I don't remember him mentioning you."

"It must've been before he moved away."

"He's only in Tavernier," I say. "It's a short drive."

"Do you see him often?"

I shut my mouth. My shoulders instinctively stiffen. My father and I have been somewhat estranged since he recovered from the prostate cancer. It was before college. Right around the time I started hanging around with Yaurena, and he moved. "It's been such a nice night," I say. "Carla, are you ready to go?"

I turn to look at her and for the first time notice the tension in her neck and eyes. She's rigid. With one palm, she smooths a wrinkle on her dress, then says, "A few minutes. Wait for me at the car."

Air conditioning stirs a loose hair from beneath my bun. Heat leeches my skin. I turn to her. "Excuse me?"

"We're having a private conversation," Jim says. "If you don't mind."

Rage takes over my body. I don't even look at Carla. I can't. My heart pounds in my ears and I feel suddenly like I could really kill someone. But the Monroe County sheriff is here, and so is the guy that runs the detention center in Key West. I wipe my palms on my pants and smile. "Enjoy your private conversation in private, then." I clap Jim so hard on the shoulder that he physically recoils. "Nice meeting you, Jimbo."

I turn and walk away without saying anything else.

• • •

The night before my mom left, I was working in the gardens with Mimi. We had a big lot—three acres of green land just below the hills. The space was on an incline so we couldn't grow much but herbs. Even at that age, I knew the difference between sage and lemon balm, chive, parsley, and thyme. I liked the feeling of the dirt on my skin, all moist and smooth. Mimi said I was like a weed—the sun and dirt kept pushing me taller.

I was watering a square of thyme when my mom showed up. She rode around most days in an old Yamaha motorized scooter. The front plate hung crooked from where she ran into a tree one night, drunk. I stared at her as she putted in. The motor made a sound like our old generator when the power was out.

"What are you looking at?" Mom asked.

She was a very short woman, stick thin, and the complete opposite of Dad with his dark hair and eyes. Mom was Irish with red hair and yucky colored freckles. She never took well to the sunlight in Montserrat. Dad said she got in trouble across the pond and that was why she was stuck here now. "Hi Mama," I said.

She stared at me. "Why are you always dirty? Eliza, why does my child always look like this?"

"It's good for her," Mimi said. "She grows like a weed."

"Ladies don't play in the dirt."

"Ladies don't buy dope, either." Mimi stopped her weeding

and stood at the edge of the yard, rake in hand. She was beautiful. Her eyes were calm, and that was part of what made her beautiful. Mimi entering a room could stop any man or woman in their tracks.

Mom was quiet. Then she kicked down the kickstand of her scooter and stalked over to Mimi, her shoes dislodging the newly planted sage seeds I'd just finished. Her face was red, like it always was, and for a moment I got really scared. I'd seen Mom like this before—raging mad and spitting curse words but usually at Dad. Mimi was smaller than Dad, not as strong. "Excuse me?" Mom asked.

Mimi stayed calm and silent. I got that feeling in my stomach, only I couldn't recognize it back then. I just knew I felt like I needed to go to the bathroom but couldn't. "Mimi," I said.

"Stay there," she called.

I stayed where I was, watching. They were far enough away that I could hear the angry pitch of their voices but not what they were saying. Mom's eyes were open wide, shiny like glass and her mouth was moving fast. Mimi was just calm.

I sat in the dirt. It was warm and moist from a recent rain. I pulled my knees up to my chest and stared at Mom. Go away, I said in my mind. Go away, far away. Go away, far away. Go away, far away. I clenched my hands. I stared hard. They talked some more. Mimi smiled. Finally, Mom moved away from Mimi. She hunched over and made a puking noise, her hands on her belly.

Mimi watched her, then turned to look at me.

I sat in the dirt with my hands clenched and sweat pouring down my face.

TWENTY

Carla can barely speak on the ride home. Her heart races as they speed up Route 1. Eli is driving and she shouldn't be. Eli is spending the night and she shouldn't be. None of this should've happened between them. People have picked up on things between her and Eli and now her shot has been jeopardized.

This can't happen. She lived through it during grade school and her life is never going to be like that again.

Tightness prickles her chest, so strong she feels like she's having a heart attack. Arcs of pain shoot out from her ribcage. Carla clutches her chest; her Xanax is at home. Even in the air conditioning of the car, beads of sweat form and she has to focus on breathing.

"What is it?" Eli finally says. She spent the first half of the ride fuming in silence. "Did he upset you?" Carla is quiet. "Carla?"

"I need to get home." She clutches her chest tighter, thinking of the way Jim leaned into her. He smelled like money—that smell that rich men get. She's wanted his endorsement for months now. He's the kind of person that carries others once he believes in them. His endorsement wouldn't just mean campaign money and a win, it would mean entering the top circle in the Keys, a group she's never had access to.

"Is it a panic attack?" Eli asks.

"Eli..."

"I'm driving as fast as I can," she says. "What happened?"

Carla fixes one of the air vents so it's blowing directly on her face, then leans back in the chair. Palm trees race by. They've just passed over the Seven Mile Bridge, headed south, and the stink of sea grass and salt grows thicker as they pass through Bahia

Honda State Park. She tries to breathe deeply. "It was nothing. I'm fine."

"What did he say?"

The pain is worse than normal, and for a moment she wonders what would happen if she died right here in this car. It's pitch black outside, barely any stars. If she didn't know this road so well, she could believe they were anywhere—maybe Vegas or California. She wouldn't mind. Maybe, that would even be better. "He didn't say anything about me. He said something about you."

Eli's eyes flicker to hers. Her shoulders stiffen, then she leans back in the driver's seat. "People say shit about me all the time," she says. "What's new about that?"

"He was worried about my campaign. He said we work too closely and you might be limiting my votes in certain areas."

Eli lets out something that sounds like a laugh, but isn't. It makes Carla feel like shit. Worse shit than she already feels. "Well, you might actually get some gay votes because of me. You're welcome."

"Eli—"

"People have never liked me in Marathon. Why do you care?"

Carla looks outside the window. She hates this. She hates confrontation. Her mother always said it was funny how upset she'd get over fights when she's always been aggressive. "You don't understand."

"You're not actually listening to this guy. Are you?"

The tightness and burning in her chest moves to her neck. Carla tries to focus on breathing but all she can sense is Eli's perfume. Eli's shampoo. The heat of her body. The way her glare lingers as she drives down the road. "Wait until we get to the house."

"Why?"

"Focus on driving."

"What? You're just going to throw me away?"

The pain fissures in her chest. A dark, ugly feeling jars loose inside her. She turns to Eli. "You did all this because you wanted to get in bed with me. Everyone knows that."

Eli goes stiff, still. Then suddenly she yanks on the steering wheel and slams on the breaks. The car slows and she pulls onto the side of the road, the truck behind them blaring a warning. Finally, they stop. Carla's heart races. She feels like she can't take another second of this. Life just needs to go back to the way it was—easy. No election, no worries. She needs to be with Jeb. He was fine and no one asked questions, no one gave her second looks.

"Eli, I need to go home."

"Fuck you. You don't get to talk to me like that."

"This is exactly what Jim said you'd do."

"Jim is a racist, homophobic asshole who hates anyone who's different from him." Outside is black. Swollen with darkness. They're less than ten miles from her house. "He's doing this because I'm not part of that group. You know that."

"It's your attitude," Carla says, and Eli gives a dramatic exhale. "He's always been nice to me."

Eli leans forward against the steering wheel. She's quiet for several moments before Carla realizes she's crying. When she first realizes it, heat rushes to her face. Then she gets that tightness in her chest, the same way she did that night when Eli was sick. She leans forward and touches Eli's hand, but Eli snatches it away. The sound of her breathing fills the car. "Do you want me to go away?" Eli asks.

"No," Carla says immediately. "I would never want that."

But in her mind, she replays Jim's words.

You're not tied to her. Are you? We all know how she is. Those types of people you just can't trust.

TWENTY-ONE

I get myself together enough to drop Carla off and leave immediately after. While she hesitates before getting out of the car,
she doesn't try to stop me. She doesn't apologize. I'm still crying. I haven't cried like this in ages, not since Yaurena left for
California. Back then I swore to myself I would never cry like this
again, and I did pretty good for a while.

I get home around eleven pm and turn the central air on high.
I'm sweating and peel off my tux. I leave the pieces scattered
across the floor, pad over to the refrigerator in my bra and underwear, the cold air springing goosebumps to my damp skin. It
smells faintly stale.

I sit there, fuming, when my phone lights up.

you don't know what it's like. i can't talk to you about this

I clench my hands.

it's different for you

I throw the phone on the couch where a yellow glow illuminates it for several seconds before falling dark again. My stomach aches something fierce. I stand up and grab my soy candle
again, light it. Shadows dance across the walls of the apartment
and soon the smell of the vanilla in the soy has overwhelmed the
staleness. I pull out a large t-shirt from my overnight bag. It's
brown with a tear near the bottle hem—a Redskins shirt. Carla's.
I bring it to my nose and breathe in deep. It smells like her shampoo. Like the sterile clean of her house.

•••

The next day, I call Carla but she doesn't answer. I give her all day
and then call again. No answer. I text her, but she doesn't text
back. The feeling in my stomach grows stronger. It's beautiful

outside—the water is turquoise, glowing in the sunlight and the birds are singing.

When Yaurena left me, there were no goodbyes, either. The Sunday before her husband packed them up and moved them, she came over to my apartment. She wore a sundress, the kind of thing an eighth grader would wear for a prom, even though she was old enough to be an eighth grader's mother. It was grey and blue. She had a headband in her black hair.

"I can't come inside," she said.

"Yes, you can." She lingered on my stoop for several seconds before turning back to look at her car—it was a Mercedes. Black. Then she passed by me and entered the tiny apartment. The hallway was so narrow that when she turned to face me, we almost bumped into one another. "What is it?" I asked. "You didn't say you were coming over."

Yaurena stared at me. I hated the stupid headband she wore. It made her look childish. I reached up and slipped it off her. Her hair fell, slick with her hair gel, around her angular face. "I didn't know I needed to ask permission."

I leaned against the wall. "What, then?" She didn't say anything, just leaned into me and pressed her mouth to my own. Yaurena was a walking contradiction—soft, almost mesmerized by my presence at times, then other times acting out spitefully like I was the root of all her problems. Her hands went to my pants, moving fast, even for her. "What? What happened, Rena?"

She didn't answer me. Her mouth fell to my throat. Her skin was damp, like she ran to get here, and we fucked right there in the hallway on the wood floor. I had bruises on my knees for weeks afterwards. That was the last time I saw her.

•••

After a week of not hearing from Carla, I stop updating the Facebook page and website. Work has been smooth—more business than usual. I start getting up early in the mornings to run

90

and workout. There's so much more time now. I drive home and sit at the table wondering what to do with myself.

Everything comes to a head when I see her at a Business Guild meeting early the next month. I haven't been sleeping very well but at least I look good. All the exercise has trimmed off the soft layer of fat along my hips and lower abdomen. I feel empty in the way that I don't care anymore, dangerous like I could light a building on fire and not feel anything.

I get to the Guild luncheon late and sit down next to the state attorney, Jeannette. Wiry black curls spring from her head. Her large glasses make her eyes look like marbles, waxing open at me as I settle in the seat. She has about five months left on her tenure and then she's up for re-election. Most of us know she won't win. That's why I like her. She pats my back as I drape a napkin in my lap.

Across the room, I find Carla seated at a table with a bunch of younger real estate agents. They're all blonde, all curvy. Honestly, they all look pretty much the same except for Carla. She wears dark clothes while they all wear tropical colors, wedge sandals, and dangly earrings. Her hair is black and she isn't as tan as the rest of them. She sits with her back ramrod straight. Her lips purse.

"You okay?" Jeannette asks. She hands me a small flyer for a barbeque next week. A meet and greet for Carla sponsored by Jim, the hotel owner.

I run my fingers around the edge of the paper. Fire takes over my chest, branching outward until my hands start to feel numb. Fucking Jim. I should've known from the beginning. I place the flyer back on the table, and look at Jeannette. "Looks like fun."

"They did you dirty, huh?"

I laugh. "I'm just glad I know a good lawyer."

"That's alright, honey." She leans back in her chair. "You're young. This is nothing for you."

I stare out across the room. There's a smell from the buffet, something like quiche or cheese. I wrinkle my nose and stab at a piece of chocolate mousse cake a waiter has placed in front of me. I'm deep into the frosting part when I spot Carla rising from her seat. I look away immediately, feeling stupid that I've even come here. Besides Jeannette and one or two others, I'm not friendly with anyone. And even Jeannette—I don't know her husband's name or where she lives. I don't know anything about her, really, except that she's as forward and as carefully avoided as I am.

I'm about to shove a bite of cake in my mouth when I sense movement behind me. It's in my blind spot, so I'm caught off guard. Then warm hands are on my shoulders and Carla's there, leaning down. I know because of the shampoo, the faint tang scent of her laundry detergent. She places a soft kiss on my cheek.

Fork halfway to my mouth, I freeze. Then, as quickly as she swooped in, she's gone again.

I manage to get through the end of the meeting but by the time the President adjourns, I can barely stand to be in the room anymore. I sit several moments longer than necessary waiting for everyone to clear out. Carla lingers as I predicted. She takes a couple of photos with the local photographer. They talk like they like each other, like they're friends.

The chocolate cake has left a film of sugary sweetness over my teeth. I wet my finger and rub them clean, nodding at a few people heading out. I just want them to leave. I just want it to be me and Carla—that's the only way things ever felt like they made sense here—but at the same time, I want her to hurt. I want to know why.

Finally, the crowd around her dissipates. I stand up and head over to where Carla is. She gathers her things and is picking up her bag when she sees me. She stops. Her eyes go to my face, then drop to the floor. "Eli."

"Should I tell you to fuck off here? Or should we go somewhere more private?"

She looks around. Outwardly, she seems fine. Her clothes are clean and not wrinkled. Her hair has been straightened and she has on makeup. But her skin holds a pallor. She appears duller than the last time we spoke. "Please don't take this personally."

"So you're not fucking Jim now?"

Carla turns scarlet. She pulls her purse over her shoulder and glares at me before starting for the door. I follow close behind. There are still a few people around, but no one that matters. I keep quiet until we're in the parking garage outside the hotel conference room and her wedges echo on the concrete.

"Carla?"

"I really can't," she says. "You always do this."

"Do what?"

She stops at her car and holds out her key to open the front door. Her hand shakes. The car beeps and then she opens the door. "You're always lecturing me."

"I was literally hired to lecture you."

She puts her purse on the passenger's seat and turns to me but doesn't meet my gaze. A faint sheen of perspiration clings to her forehead. She wants me go away. I can tell. It's like I'm an embarrassment, a reminder of something she wanted once but doesn't anymore. "I hope you'll still support me."

A burning sensation settles in my stomach. I want to laugh but I can't. "Are you serious? Why should I?"

She opens her mouth, then closes it again. The heat swarms around me, so thick and wet I feel like I'm suffocating.

• • •

That evening, I invite Lindsay over to make me feel better. We met several years ago at Roostica where she works as a GM and occasional bartender. Sometimes I'll call when I need her. She doesn't always show up but she agrees to come over tonight— her air conditioning is being fixed and she's not working. It's late by the time she gets to my place. The sunset is purple, clouds tinted pink. She wears a blue and white paisley romper that's too youthful for a woman in her early forties. Her breasts spill out the top.

She holds out a six pack to me.

"Thoughtful," I say. I take the pack and place it in the fridge, remove two of the beers and pop them open. Carla would never do this. She'd never show up just to hang out, not unless there was something strategic in it for her.

"What's with you, Eli?"

"Nothing."

I place the beer on the counter for Lindsay. I like her fine—she's a short woman with a great rack, long brown hair and a hard look to her chin and cheekbones. I'm not particularly into her but she's easy and attractive in a raw, dangerous kind of way. I lean into her and she smirks. "No small talk today?"

I take one of her romper straps between my fingers, pull it off her shoulder. Then the other. The fabric sags, revealing a white, lace bra. Skimming one hand to her back, I undo the clasp. Her bra straps slip down her arms. I lean forward and kiss the top of one breast. "Not today, love."

I pull the bra all the way down, exposing her nipples. She's darker colored than Carla—her areolas are more brown than pink. She's rounder, too. No kids, no breastfeeding. I skim my palm over one nipple and she reacts immediately, pulling me closer to her. She's pretty but not that pretty. When she kisses me, I don't feel anything.

•••

Lindsay smells like lime and tonic. Splayed out on the bed, her eyes close. She's more firm than soft. I lick my way down her thighs. They're not small but not what I'm used to, either. There's less to hold onto. My mouth keeps searching for those stretch marks, the thin white threads, but there's nothing. Just smooth, cool skin. I wish she would scream, pant, like Carla does. She seems so sure of herself, her legs pulled back, bent at the knees, completely open to me. I want her to hide herself, to be unsure. I want her to fight at first, then lose control completely. I want her breasts to slope and her fingers to be smaller, her nails shorter. I want her to wear a scar along her jawline, and stare down at me like she loves me when I kiss her belly.

···

The next morning, I call Mimi and head up to Miami. I drink from an IPA bottle on the way up. Route 1 is quiet in the summer. Palm fronds dust the highway and the stench of sea grass inundates. I'm lost in thought the entire drive, the way I am all the time now. Images of Carla race through my mind—her splayed out across the bed, her in the shower, her perched over a pair of pants and ironing board. As much as I try, I can't get rid of them.

I barely notice I'm driving until I reach Mimi's condo. I hate where she lives. The building is one of six, all tall and square and without any character. There's about a thousand cars in the parking lot and a fake pond in the middle. The outside of the building is painted perfect peach. Since it's Miami and I've arrived in the afternoon, a rainstorm drenches me on my way in. Thunder booms outside as I take the elevator to the thirteenth floor.

Her hall is painted a deep red color and a gold and maroon carpet lines the floor up to her condo entrance. I knock three times and wait. It's been months since I last saw my grandmother. It was early February and she was visiting for my birthday.

I exhale as she opens the door. A gust of scent, incense, wafts out at me. Light seems to ball around her. "Pet," Mimi says, peeking out from the door. She wears a muumuu which I generally find unacceptable, but this one is cute—white with green swirls on it. Her blonde hair is pulled back tight in a bun. She smiles and opens her arms.

"I'm here," I say.

She pulls me into a hug. Her skin is warm, soft and yielding like she's always been, but she feels smaller than the last time

I saw her. "So, what has happened?" She ushers me inside the condo. "Tell me everything."

I put my bag down on the countertop in the kitchen. It smells like salt and meat and when I look on the stove, I see she's got a pot of goat water boiling. The soup bubbles, goat meat stirring the surface, the smell of onion and spices filling the room. The smell of it reminds me of playing in the kitchen while Mimi cooked back in Montserrat, using a broom and old tennis ball like I was a cricket player. "Where did you find goat meat?" I ask, reaching for a bowl out of the cupboard.

"I wandered into someone's farm." She pads around me and gets herself a bowl.

I turn. "What?"

"I am joking, pet. What is wrong? You are skinny."

I put the bowl down. Mimi has a friendly face, friendly eyes. Not like me. I have resting bitch face. People want to go up to her and talk to her and tell her their problems. People know on instinct to stay the hell away from me. "She doesn't want me anymore," I say. "Do you have any spells to make her want me again?"

Mimi sets her bowl down. A band of light peeks in through the curtains, and in the rain, the prism of colors expands. The rainbow flashes over Mimi's arm before disappearing again. "Could you not do a spell yourself?"

"I'm only good at making people go away."

Mimi makes a tisking sound and removes a ladle from a drawer. "Why do you need her so badly? Why not someone else?"

"Why did you love Grandpa and not someone else?"

Mimi laughs. I love her laugh. It's deep and coarse from the smoking, low and beautiful. It reminds me of sunset in the evening, the kind that is red and raging. "Okay, okay," she says. "We will eat first and then we can talk about the girl."

•••

Mimi is the kind of drunk I've always wanted to be. She is

measured and cautious with her glasses of chardonnay. She drinks water in between and never gets sloppy. That's how she is now—her eyes are glossed and happy but she's calm. She shows me a new shawl she bought from a Finnish man that works near Miami Beach. Then she gives me new garnet crystals.

"If you're all powerful, Mimi, then why don't you have a man?"

She turns to look at me and the corner of her mouth curls. "Why? Should I want one?"

"I wouldn't. But I thought maybe you would."

She chuckles and lights one of the soy candles in the living room. The storm has passed. The curtains hang open, the humidity of the lingering storm presses on the windows. "Maybe my life is supposed to be like this," she says. "Anyway, I am quite happy."

We sit opposite one another on the rug in the living room, the candle flickering between us. We're not supposed to be drinking during incantations but Mimi has always indulged in wine. It's her one weakness, she's always said. Besides me. She sits up straight and closes her eyes, placing her hands on her knees and taking deep breaths for her incantations.

I remember her doing this as a child. I always thought she looked silly. I think so, now, too. She's so focused and sure of herself. A deep ache surfaces in my chest. I try to be calm and focus on the burning flame, but images of Carla keep filtering through.

TWENTY-TWO

It's hot. Carla wears a sleeveless shirt and white canvas pants to catch the breeze. What a dumb idea, having a barbeque in the summer. She could kick herself. She stands at the edge of the backyard, Jim's backyard. The petunias bloom and it smells like cough syrup. Everything is beautiful and perfect and feels completely wrong. She forces a smile as Jim sidles up to her.

"Are you enjoying yourself?" he asks.

She shifts. Sweat chafes her thighs. "This is amazing, Jim. Thank you."

"You seem a little uncomfortable."

A server passes by them and Jim snatches a pink, fizzing drink in a champagne glass. He holds it out to her. Carla smiles. "No, thank you."

"Come on, Carla."

"I'm not drinking until the election is over."

Jim is silent for a moment and Carla feels that stirring sensation in her chest again, the one she gets right before a panic attack. She's been having them more and more frequently now. Waking up in the middle of the night, rolling over in bed, and finding it empty.

Jim sips from the champagne flute.

"Has she been bothering you?" he asks.

Pain in her chest again. "Who?"

"Your former campaign manager."

Above them, a large gumbo limbo tree shifts, providing a moment of shade. Carla wants to stand in a cold shower. She pictures Eli here standing next to her, one hand on her back. All cool and comfortable like she always is. "I don't see her anymore," Carla says.

"Good. It's best you aren't around her."

The breeze picks up. In the dead of summer like this, Carla's allergies act up. She can feel them now—the burning at the back of her throat, itchy eyes. Pollen coats the air, swells in it. Like the salt. Heavy. "She's a decent person," Carla says. "I don't have a problem with her."

Jim is quiet, sipping whatever is in the flute. He has a prominent Adam's apple. So did her ex. "She's not the type that my colleagues or I would ever associate with."

Carla stills. Sweat pinches at her skin. She feels like she is coated in alabaster and quickly drying.

• • •

"This is just the way things are," her father said once. She was thirteen and had just gotten beaten up by a fifteen-year-old at her school. She walked into the kitchen at home after getting off the school bus with a black eye and busted lip. Her father told her to get a pack of frozen peas from the freezer and apply it to her eye. The lip she washed in the sink and applied salve to.

She sat in the kitchen as her older brother played outside, her father working under the kitchen sink, wrench in hand. "It hurts," she said. "Mary got me hard this time."

Her father kept working. His hands were dirty and the smell of grease lingered in the small space. One of the tiles on the floor was cracked from where her brother dropped a pint of canned baked beans last week. "How come Mary hates you so much?"

Carla shifted at the table, head pounding. "She says she hates girls with hand-me-downs."

"Those ain't even hand-me-downs."

"That's what I told her. Iris is the one with those."

Her father was silent for a moment before wrenching a bolt loose on the sink with a satisfied grunt. "So, stop being friends with Iris," he said. "Be friends with Mary instead. Then she can't pick on you anymore."

Carla placed the pack of peas back on the table. It was cold outside, the dead of winter in upstate New York. Frost kissed the window above the sink. She thought about being friends with Mary, and what that would be like. Maybe she could go to the thrift shop and get some tight jeans like the rest of them had and then borrow some makeup from her brother's girlfriend. "What about Iris?"

Her father placed the wrench on the ground and sat up. Sweat ran down his face in lines, even in the cool air of the kitchen. His cheeks were red like soil, stained from the wind. "Hell, if you want to keep getting black eyes, then stay friends with her."

TWENTY-THREE

I wake up in the morning and Mimi isn't in the kitchen or her bedroom. I find a note on the kitchen counter.

went to get some papaya. hot cakes in the oven

The apartment is silent, much too large for just her. I pad across the kitchen and turn on the oven so the hot cakes will heat up. They're my favorite besides goat water, like sweetened corn bread. Mimi's also left some icing in a container on the table.

I investigate the cupboards while the hot cakes are warming up. It smells like vanilla extract, that sharp, sweet flavor. On the refrigerator is a picture of me with my father back in Montserrat. The volcano stretches behind us, a set of rolling green fields in between. My father wears a thin, cotton sweater that, after seeing himself in the photo, he started calling a fag sweater and threw it out.

The timer on the oven dings and I take the hot cakes out. I slice them in half and place two on my plate. Steam wafts off them in waves. I drip icing on top, then bring a piece to my mouth. The smell and taste of them has always reminded me of pancakes, but not the texture.

On the kitchen countertop, my phone lights up. I check the screen.

I don't know how things got like this
Carla.
I'm going to lose this election

For a second, I just stare at the phone in anger. Bitch, I think. Fucking bitch with her perfect hair and ass and always getting everything she wants. I pick up my phone. *How is that my problem?*

A few seconds pass. Then, *i am really starting not to care*

I'm not sure what that means so I try to go back to eating—the hot cakes are perfect, warm, moist, like birthday cake—but a sudden cold feeling has taken over my body. Next to me, sunlight spots the floor, crawling in through the blinds. It's a beautiful morning. Tiptoeing around the spots of sunlight, I open the cupboard with all the alcohol and pour myself a mug full of old coffee and Bailey's and stick it in the microwave. Before it's done heating, I pick up my phone again. *Dinner next week.*

I wait. A few minutes pass by, then, *let's meet at roostica on thursday*

Okay, I reply.

Sunlight hits the glass funny, the way it did yesterday, and the prism of rainbow light appears once more. I think about Carla. Her legs and hips, the way she snores lightly before falling into deeper sleep.

A prism of colored light crosses the wall opposite me before shrinking and slivering away.

• • •

Mimi comes back around eleven and forces me to go to a local bakery with her. She drives us there in her little red convertible, the top down and sunshine pouring in. It makes me laugh; she's so incredibly proud of the car, smiling at pedestrians when we stop at stop signs and examining the expressions of other drivers.

She parks on the corner of a large lot and we walk several yards to enter the bakery. "Pet, look at those," she says as we peruse the refrigerated display. Their cakes are beautiful —six-inch white cakes with blue icing, twelve inch chocolate cakes with red and pink frosted flowers. Every single one of them is perfect, icing in thin ridges and large swirls.

"They're nice," I say. "But I don't think we need an entire cake."

We shuffle forward in the long line. The shop is small and bright with white walls and lace curtains over the windows. It smells like sugar and plastic. Mimi leans into my shoulder. "What about her?" she asks. "The girl at the counter."

I turn, focus on the cashier. She's young—just a bit older than me with reddish-blonde hair and a nose ring. The ring, for me, is an immediate turn off. She does have nice breasts, though. They round over the top of her apron. She smiles. Open and happy. I look at her and feel nothing. "She's too young for me."

"Eliza—"

"Mimi, come on. Let's just get some cannolis, okay?"

Mimi sighs. She wraps her arms around my bicep and holds. Ever since I grew taller than her, she's held me like this. Like if she didn't, I'd forget I was made of her. "I think you should move to Miami."

The line moves forward. The cash register dings. "What? Why?"

"Because..." she squeezes tighter. "Your energy is all wrong in the Keys. You should be here, close to me."

"I'm not ready to leave."

A woman brushes past me. She's got a big, perfect ass and long, dark hair. Finely drawn eyebrows. Probably Cuban. There are a lot of Cuban women here. All of them are incredibly good looking and most likely all straight. "I watched your father fall apart for your mother," Mimi says. For an old lady, her grip is like stone. "I will not let that happen again."

We're almost at the counter now. The reddish-blonde girl looks up, sees Mimi and waves. Mimi chuckles and waves back. Then the girl's eyes move to mine. I look at her, searching for a hint of darkness, a spark, but there's nothing. "What would I even do up here?" I ask.

"The same thing you do down there, pet."

"I don't know anyone here. How would I get clients?"

Mimi pats my arm. At the counter, she orders two cannolis and lets go of my arm to reach for her purse. "Easy," she says. "I tell people and they will come. Just think on it. Yes?"

I manage to remove a twenty-dollar bill from my pocket before Mimi finds her debit card. Smirking, I hand the bill to the cashier. She smiles at me when our hands meet, almost shyly, and I find myself wondering what she'd be like in bed. If she'd scream and claw or if she'd just be silent, like there's nothing inside of her at all.

•••

I leave Mimi's soon after and get home to find the old couple arguing downstairs. It's strange—they never fight. I do laundry and pretend not to hear them, but even as night settles, the fight radios into my room.

Lots of strange things happen that next week. First, I gain two clients in the Miami area. The Miami guys are big hitters, people Mimi apparently plays poker with. They want website design and marketing for their law firms. It's a good catch. Second, I lose a client in the Keys, a doctor in Summerland Key who knows Jim. Third, when I'm shopping in the Key Plaza Publix, I pass a group of women who all stop what they were doing to glare at me.

And then there's Carla.

She sits at the Roostica bar when I walk in on Thursday. She's in my least favorite clothes—grey trousers that pinch near her hips and a white blouse that does nothing to show off her bust. Her back is straight. Impeccable posture. I weave through the tables to get to her.

I have most of my business meetings here. The restaurant is dimly lit with drawings of wine and grape vines and Italian food across the wall. It smells like garlic and butter. I sit down at the bar next to Carla and take off my sweater.

"You're late," she says.

I look up. The bartender tonight is Lindsay. I could almost laugh. "Hey, Lindsay."

"Hey," she says. "Fullsail?"

"Yes, please."

I turn to look at Carla. She's sitting face forward, not looking at me, but her mouth is open slightly, her jaw locked. She looks tired. Her eyes lack the wanting I'm used to seeing—they just look dead. Her lips are painted, and she's put blush on. "Do you know her?" she asks.

"Intimately," I say, and smile at the look of hurt that flashes across her face. "So, what can I do for you, Carla?"

Lindsay brings me a Fullsail in a glass. Carla shifts. "I shouldn't be doing this."

"What? Being seen with me?"

"I shouldn't be talking to you."

"I know," I say. "I'm such bad news."

Carla lets out a hiss of irritation and it sends a jolt of pleasure straight to my belly. She takes a sip of her water, playing with the ring of condensation the glass leaves on the bartop. "This was never going to happen," she says. "You know that."

"It happened just fine for a while."

Carla is quiet. The smell of her shampoo wafts out as she shifts on the chair. I glance down; her pants pull tight around the top of her thighs. "It wouldn't last."

"Why not?"

She exhales. "Eli, please."

Lindsay returns, asking us what we want to eat. I order a mini-pizza with olives. Carla gets a salad. It feels wrong to be here with her, in a place so public. I want to be at her house with her, watching her putz around in the kitchen barefoot with her hair loose and no makeup. I want to be able to touch her, to see her eyes. I want her all around me, her rage and her softness both.

"I think I'm at a stalemate with Johnny Dogger," she says.

"So get Jimbo to pull some strings."

She makes a face. "Jim's not... he doesn't work like that."

"Too bad. What's he good for, then?"

Waitresses pass behind us. The room has grown full now—voices rise and fall. In the large mirror above the bar, I watch the couples that pass through the door. I know some of them, but only by face. There's no one important here. I place my hand on

Carla's thigh. She falls still, then turns to look at me. "Being tied may not be a bad thing," she says.

"Don't you want to win?"

She makes a face, then on the bar top, her phone lights up. She reaches for it immediately and I remove my hand.

"I have to go soon," she says.

I still. The beer sweats in my hands. "I thought we were having dinner?"

"My car's in the shop."

"So? I'll bring you home."

She places her phone in her purse and takes out a twenty-dollar bill, lays it on the table. "Jeb is coming to get me."

A jolt rips through my chest. Pain, searing pain, shoots through my ribcage, worse than I've ever felt. Heat rushes to my cheeks and I look away. For a moment, I forget how to breathe. Jeb? Mr. Make America Great Again? I almost can't compute the thought. "Seriously?" I manage. "Are you fucking kidding me, Carla?"

Carla's eyes go soft. Then she turns away. Wrinkles form under her chin as she frowns. "Here's a twenty. That should cover it."

Something in me shatters. I take the twenty she's placed on the table and throw it at her. It hits her chest, then drifts to the floor, spiraling like a leaf caught on a breeze. "Take your fucking money," I say. Anger bleeds from my pores. I feel like I could kill her. Like I could tie her down and squeeze her breath from her lungs. "I don't want it."

"Eli, stop it."

"Don't. And don't ever ask me for help again."

She touches my wrist and I twist violently out of her grasp. There are eyes on us now. I can feel them, but I don't care. She used me. Like Yaurena did. Used me because she was bored and needed help and now she's throwing me away.

"Don't touch me," I tell her. "Get the fuck out."

Her face colors. Her beautiful face. Her freckles, those blue eyes, all shy and withdrawn, the way I've made them. She picks the twenty up and grabs her purse. It looks like she might cry, and suddenly, for the first time, I see the age in her eyes.

It's quiet in the restaurant for a moment and then someone laughs, breaking the spell. Carla turns and leaves.

I twist away from her, facing the bar. I'm hot all over. When I pick up my beer, my hand shakes so badly I can barely drink from it. A small bit spills over the side and I put it back down again. Lindsay comes over and pours me two fingers worth of tequila in a large glass. After a couple of deep breaths, I'm able to bring the glass to my lips and down the clear liquid.

"You okay?" she asks.

My body hums. "Fine."

I feel like something inside me has been torn loose. I can't believe I let myself get duped. After Yaurena, I didn't think it could happen again. I thought I'd been through it all already.

The pizza I ordered finally comes out. It sits on the plate next to me, steaming. I remember the night after her first debate, how I tipped the delivery boy. How I watched her after she fell asleep, worried this was too much for her. So stupid.

"Eli?"

I look up. Dark brown eyes stare back at me. "I'm fine," I say. "What time do you get off?"

TWENTY-FOUR

Carla cries on the ride home.

"What?" Jeb asks. "Is it the menopause?"

She pulls her sunglasses over her eyes and looks out the window. The sun is still up—it's too early to go home. She thought she'd have at least two hours with Eli. But this is the way things are with Jeb. She never knows when he's going to show up. Usually it's when she doesn't want him to.

"My sister said she cried all the time when it happened."

Carla wipes her face, watching the trees race by as they head north on Route 1. The buttonwoods are thick with leaves this time of year. They sway in the wind, a perfect green. She wonders what Bahia Honda looks like now—it's been two years since she last visited the park. Swimming and paddle boarding were the two reasons she moved down here. She rarely does either, anymore.

"Fuck," Jeb continues. "What the fuck, Carla."

"Just drive," she snaps and suddenly her whole body is on fire. Like ants running under her skin. Jeb doesn't get what this campaign has been like. Eli doesn't, either. Politics are just like this, and if Eli's not tough enough to understand that, then it's really not her problem. She wipes her face again. Her cheeks are hot. Beads of sweat condense on her neck.

"Should've left your ass at Roostica," he says. "What are you doing eating there, anyway? Everyone knows that place is for fags."

"The sheriff eats there."

"My point."

Irritation rises inside her. It's been like this since the start of the campaign. It's like she has no control over anything in her life anymore. Carla looks down at her feet. Fresh car mats dispense the smell of rubber. Jeb's car is new. A GMC Sierra. 5.3 liter V8. She memorized the specs when he was looking. "Call Billy Talc later and ask him to come have dinner one night with us."

"Why?"

"Because I want him to vote for me."

Jeb shifts in the driver's seat. He's got his legs spread open, wide as they can get, and for a moment, it reminds her of how Eli sits. "Babe, he's more of a guy you take fishing. I ain't gonna ask him to dinner."

Heat flies to her face. She stares at him. Eli's words come floating through her mind. *What's he good for then?* Carla unbuttons the top button of her blouse. She turns the AC vents so they're directly on her, then unbuttons the next button. Cool air slides between her breasts. She shivers. "Invite him," she says. "If he doesn't want to come, he won't."

Jeb is silent for a moment, then turns to look at her. His eyes flicker down to her cleavage, then back up. "Is it true what Jimmy thinks? You was boning the dyke girl?" They pass Boca Chica. Jets boom overhead, then fade out. "I don't care if you was, Carla." He touches her leg. She feels tired, achy. "Okay, I'll ask Billy tomorrow."

The heat of his palm presses in through her jeans. He smells like sweat and salt air, the way he always smells, and something burns inside her chest, just above where her heart is.

•••

Jeb loans her his old Corvette so she can get up early for work in the morning. But that night, she can't fall asleep. She lies in bed for two hours thinking about Eli, about the election, before turning the lights back on and climbing out of bed. She sweats. She's tried everything—hot tea, a warm shower, even a half a Xanax. It feels like Eli is there with her in the house. The smell of her lingers somehow.

At one am, she gets in the Corvette and starts to drive. The windows are down. Warm air blows into the cab of the old car. Even though there's sweat rolling down her back, she is calm.

At this point, she's not even sure she wants to win the election anymore. The public speaking aspect has kept her up at night. She hates it. And ninety percent of the time, she's making things up. It's not how it was when Eli was helping her.

Palm trees fly by. It's been a while since it rained, and the grass yellows, the tarmac blackened with heat. The tides are low. From the glove compartment, she fishes out the spare pack of Marlboros Jeb keeps. Leaning into the dash, away from the wind, she lights it with one hand and sucks the smoke into her lungs.

Before she even knows what she's doing, she turns onto the road to Eli's house, passing under the tilted streetlamps, humming with electricity. She slows near the end of the street, then pulls into the spot beneath Eli's house. Her car is there alone.

Good.

Carla climbs out of the car and starts for the stairs. She's not nervous, just hot. The heat seems to swarm around her. Heat in the night. You can't get away from it down here. Even at two in the morning.

After taking the last step, she stops. Up here, in the soft light from the streetlamp, she can just barely make out the edge of the water. It looks black. Shimmering like oil. There's nothing in the Big Coppitt bay but bacteria and sharks.

Carla raises a hand and knocks.

TWENTY-FIVE

I'm startled by the sound of knocking. Lindsay has just left so I figure it's her again. I'm in a sports bra and work out shorts when I open the door. "Hey, did you—" I stop immediately upon seeing Carla there. My entire body floods with shock. I stand up straight. Then the anger gets to me, the heat. "What the hell are you doing here?"

She checks over her shoulder, unsure. "Let me in."

"It's two in the morning."

"The light was on."

I stare at her. "Did you wait out there until Lindsay left?"

Her face scrunches up. "Who?" She looks past me, into the apartment. My clothes are on the floor by the couch. "Oh," she says, and her neck gets red. "We need to talk."

I stare at her. She's wearing those stupid yoga pants again, the ones that show off her giant, perfect ass and make me want to rip her clothing off. I wonder if there will ever be a time where I don't look at her and want to make her mine. "How'd you get here if your car's in the shop?"

I close the door behind us. She turns to look at me. "You were mean."

"I said how I feel."

"Just because you're not getting your way doesn't mean I'm a bad person."

I force a laugh and go to the refrigerator, popping open a can of Budweiser. I drink deeply, it warms my stomach. I turn to face her. "You use people."

"I don't," she says loudly. A vein in her forehead strains.

The central air comes on. Good thing, too. I'm burning up. "You used me, Carla."

Carla's eyes stay on mine. I can feel her fuming but there's another emotion beneath it. One that's soft and unsure. It makes me love her again. It makes me want to hurt her, too. Pull that t-shirt off her and twist it around her throat, squeeze and squeeze. I tilt back the beer and wait for her to deny me, but she doesn't. Instead she takes a few steps into me. She smells like cigarette smoke. She touches the fading nail marks on my shoulder. There is something loose in her, something brazen. "You just fucked her, didn't you?"

"So?"

Her mouth tightens. "You look awful."

"I look good," I say.

Carla's chest rises and falls rapidly. The t-shirt she wears is too small for her and I can see the outline of her bra under it. I reach out, tracing over the lines. Then I grab the bottom of the shirt and pull her closer to me. She stumbles and my nose bumps her forehead. When she pulls back, her eyes rise to meet mine.

• • •

She smells like soap and cigarettes and her skin tastes like sweat. She's sweet and docile under my hands. Her eyes stay on me the entire time; her chest rising and falling. I take her nipple in my mouth and bite down, then suck hard. Blood tangs my mouth.

"Eli."

I look up. Her pupils are dilated and sweat coats her brow, seeping into her hairline. I stop. With one hand, I reach up and press my palm to her throat. She exhales. Her pulse throbs. Carefully, I tighten my grasp. Carla makes a small noise before falling quiet, her eyes wide, lips mussed. A strand of hair sticks to her cheek. I squeeze tighter, tighter. Her breath grows ragged and her cheeks branch red with color. I wonder if it hurts, what it feels like. If it's worse than how I felt this evening after she left.

If my hands will leave marks and people will know I've touched her. That we were together, at least once.

Finally, she grabs my wrist. Her eyes are shiny but she's not crying, she never cries. Not for me or anyone else. I let go of her throat and place my hand on her chest. Her heartbeat is so rapid it reminds me of the beating of a butterfly's wings.

TWENTY-SIX

Carla has never been the cuddling type. She hated cuddling with Miles' father. He was too hot. That and her naturally warm body in the heat of the Keys made her feel like screaming every time he touched her. Eli's not a big cuddler, either. She'll sleep with a hand on Carla's neck or stomach but nothing else.

Tonight, she does neither.

Carla exhales. She lies on her side, cradling her head in one hand as she stares down at Eli's sleeping form. It's early in the morning now, around four am, but she can't rest. Moonlight illuminates the window, shining down on Eli. One hand is on her stomach, the other on her side. She lays on her back. Silent.

Carla touches Eli's chest. Her ribcage is faintly visible under her skin. She touches each bone, then her hand slides to Eli's stomach. Taut and tight.

Eli's eyes flutter open. She looks up at Carla. Blinks. "You okay?"

Carla stays there, resting with her head in her hand. She doesn't want to leave this moment. After tonight, things won't be the same anymore. She doesn't know why she feels like this, she just does. It won't be nice anymore, it'll just be sad and difficult. "I can't sleep."

Eli rubs her eyes. She sits up in bed and grabs a Gatorade from the nightstand, drinks. After she's done, she offers some to Carla. It's the blue kind, and tastes like chemicals. Carla takes one sip and hands it back.

Eli smooths out the sheets, then reaches for Carla. "Come here," she says.

A smile creeps over Carla's mouth. "No."

Eli's eyes go dark, and Carla gets that familiar sensation of uncertainty. But then she lightens. She grabs Carla by the arm and yanks her closer. They tussle. Eventually she ends up cradled in Eli's arms, draped across her body and out of breath. She feels stupid and young. Like she's not in her life. It's a nice sensation, one she feels is quickly moving out of her grasp. "That'll teach you," Eli says.

"Teach me what?" Carla asks.

Eli stares down at her. She traces Carla's lips then kisses her in a gentle way that's completely unlike her. Carla stiffens, then let's herself lean into the kiss. She's seen this happen before. This is how people get at the end of something. They either go hard and impenetrable or soft and gentle.

She never thought things would end like this.

Finally, Eli pulls away. "That'll teach you not to tell me no," she says.

Carla smiles and closes her eyes. After a few minutes, the tension fades from her body with the beat of Eli's heart beneath her.

TWENTY-SEVEN

In the morning, Carla is gone.

I wake up and light breaches the sky. It shines in through the window where I lay naked in a mess of tangled sheets. I'm exhausted. My neck hurts and my thighs are sore. Normally, I'd wake up like this and be pretty pleased with myself. This morning, I take one look at the empty bed and start to cry. I can't help it. I've woken up to an empty bed almost every single day of my life. I've imagined having a family for a decade now, and watched my peers grow to have them. I've prayed and set spells. I thought maybe, for a moment, that this one would stick.

Sunlight glints in my eyes. I pull the sheets over my head, ballooned in warmth and the smell of us.

It's like she knew something last night that I didn't know, like she was moving forward but I'm not ready to let her go just yet.

• • •

Months pass.

I fall into routine as I do so often: gym in the early morning, latte at Starbucks. Work takes up the greater part of my days. I stop going to Rotary and don't renew the lease on my office. I pay a charter plane to fly me to Dry Tortugas for the first time ever and sit in the sand alone tilting back IPAs and watching the tide fall.

I don't see Carla at all except for Guild meetings and sometimes at communal happy hours. It's like a stab in the heart every time. Her signs litter the road, so it's hard not to think about it. Early voting has passed and she's behind in the polls but not by much. On the radio, I hear she's sold a multi-million-dollar home to some CEO douche bag up on Duck Key. Her commission will be more money than I could ever think of.

By the end of October, Mimi finds an apartment for me in Miami. It's a one bedroom and half the price of the studio I currently rent. Second floor. All wood tile and a huge open window facing the city.

The two clients I picked up in Miami have referred me and now I work for three of them. They pay better than people do down here and none of them know me or my reputation. They talk to me like I know what I'm doing. Like I'm somebody.

On Halloween night, Lindsay invites me to a private costume party she's bartending for. I show up dressed as Wayne from Wayne's World to find a group of some of the richest and most important people in town. The house is immaculate and has two small pools in the front yard with walkways over them. The inside is full of expensive furniture and art deco windows that slope low over my head. Immediately upon finding the bar, Lindsay serves me a beer. She's dressed as a cat—same as just about every other single other woman here—but her suit is skin tight, and her D-cup breasts are cinched in a low-cut V at the front.

"No offense," I say, "but you look terrible. We should probably just leave."

A slow smile takes over her face. "Fuck off. Go find a friend."

The beer is fancy—some German IPA in a bottle. It tastes good, too. I bring it to my lips while scanning the room, unsure why she invited me to a party like this. The city mayor is here, as well as the head of the school board, the richest man in Key Haven, and two of the women that run the local news station. I feel ridiculously out of place, as I always do now. Sometimes, in the car, I cry because I hate it here. And then I cry harder because I'm going to leave soon.

"Eliza, isn't it?"

I turn. Behind me is a man dressed in a bee costume. If he weren't so ridiculous looking, I'd say he was adorable. It takes me several moments to recognize him—Arnie Prescott, the owner of the Waterfront Brewery. "Arnie, right?"

"I knew I recognized you," he says. "You did some design work for the brewery before we opened."

"Sure did. I go by Eli, though."

He shakes my hand and I wonder why the hell he's talking to me. Arnie is a big-wig in Key West. He gets guys and girls. Money and drinks. There's nothing he wants for. But in his bee costume, his face all painted up and his eyes squinting through brown horn-rimmed glasses, it's hard to believe he's the same person. "You know Lindsay?"

"Only reason I got invited."

He chuckles. "Well, the only reason I got invited was to secure a vote. They're like vultures this time of year. It's obscene."

I eye him. "You're undecided?"

"So far. And this is Johnny Dogger's party."

"Oh, shit," I say. Carla's biggest competition. I wonder what she would say if she knew I was here.

"Oh, shit is right," he says. "What about you? I heard you're no longer on Carla's campaign."

I force a laugh and down more beer. "That's like a three-shot question."

Other guests mill about. It smells like lavender essential oils or something. Above us, a large skylight reveals clouded stars. Humidity hangs over the glass. "Well, damn," Arnie says. "I've got time. Let's drink."

• • •

Arnie and I take tequila shot for shot and after a while, I decide he's not the rich fuckhead I thought he'd be. Although he seems caught up in the number of men and women he's slept with, he makes me laugh a couple times and keeps his attention focused on me, even when the current city mayor walks by.

"I don't know," I say, "it's going to be a tough vote for me this year."

"I agree. Both are money grubbers."

I hesitate, think of Carla. I think of how terrified she looked at that open forum. Maybe being tied isn't a bad thing. "Carla's not a bad egg," I say carefully. "Between you and me, she's a hell of a lot smarter than Johnny."

Arnie tilts his head. It's hard to take him seriously in his bee costume. The outfit rounds across his stomach, making him look like a black and yellow disco ball. "Yeah?"

"It's not saying much if you know Johnny."

He lets out a girlish giggle and his eyes glimmer when he looks at me. "I like you," he says. "Too bad you only like pussycats."

I take a sip of my beer. There's still a half cask of tequila between us. It sparkles in the light, smooth as silk. I imagine Carla bringing it to her mouth, the liquid wetting her lips. I miss her so much sometimes I physically ache. "I'll probably vote for her," I say. "For Carla."

Arnie is silent a moment, then reaches forward and grabs the tequila. He pours a shot and offers it to me, then pours his own. He holds it up. "After all that, you're still going to vote for her?" He clinks his shot glass with mine. Tequila spills down his fingers. "Cheers to that, then."

TWENTY-EIGHT

The night of the election is like the night of one of her school presentations but on steroids. Carla pukes three times that morning. After stomaching some toast with butter, she makes herself a mimosa and starts to dress. Everything she tries on makes her look fat so eventually she decides on the emerald-colored shirt Eli liked so much and a black skirt that cuts off below her knees. Heels. She straightens her hair in the mirror, going through layer by layer. She refills her mimosa glass.

By noon, Jim arrives at her house. He's dressed too formally—a suit. Small dots of sweat pepper his dress shirt. He looks at her empty mimosa glass and picks it up. "Are you nervous?"

She's not used to having people over. No one except Eli and Jeb have been inside in months. "A little," she admits. "Jeb is coming over soon."

"I know. I came early so we could talk."

Carla stills. "Talk about what?"

"There are some issues I suggest you rethink right now. Just in case you win tonight."

She sits down on one of the kitchen table chairs. Her paperwork is still scattered everywhere. It smells like paper, like sand, even though she hasn't been to the beach. She's barely even talked to Miles at all. The last phone call they had was weeks ago. He seemed happy but how would she know? She needs to do better with him.

Carla forces herself to exhale. The mimosas have done a decent job of calming the fire in her chest. It's still there, though small.

"I don't think I'll win, Jim."

"You have a good chance."

"I was behind Johnny, last I heard."

Jim takes a seat opposite her. His shirt is buttoned all the way to the top and it makes him look like a bobble-head. Suddenly, she hates him. She hates his shirt and his suit and the fat that gathers under his chin. "Heard Arnie and his crew at the brewery are all voting tonight. For you."

Air from the vent nudges her hair. "What?"

"He told me your little friend talked him into it at a party. It might just put you over half."

Carla leans back in her chair. She feels like she might pass out. All the blood is in her face and neck, springing beads of sweat up under her hairline. She thinks of Eli tucked into her bed. Eli's hands, her slim fingers, the way her mouth moved, the feel of her teeth on Carla's skin.

"Carla?"

She blinks, refocuses. "Which issues did you want to review?"

He frowns and places his hand palm down on the table, raps his fingertips against the wood. "Everything okay?"

"It's fine," she says. Liar, liar. Tears sting at her eyes. There's nothing else she can do. She blinks them back, clears her throat and says, "Talk to me."

TWENTY-NINE

It's nearing eight pm and I'm driving to Carla's reveal party when Mimi calls. "Pet, do you need the movers for when you come up here?"

"Who are the movers, Mimi?"

"I don't know. People who move things for you."

I change lanes, curse. Traffic grids. I'm barely at the Key Haven intersection and already the cars are backed up. Through the speakers of my car, Mimi sounds nasally, like she's got a cold. "Did you put down the deposit I gave you?"

"Yesterday," she says. Tightness rises in my throat. I swallow. "You have been doing your incantations?"

Inching the car forward, I manage to get past the first light in Stock Island. I've been meditating almost every night. Usually, I have to press through a fit of tears first. "Most days," I tell her. Someone honks behind me. I startle. I sweat even though I have the AC on inside. That's the way the heat is down here. It has a way of working deep down into you. "I gotta go, Mimi."

"You are going to cry."

I exhale into the phone. More and more lately the tears come like this—sudden and unexpected in the car, or in the grocery shop, or sometimes at night when I'm alone. "Mimi, I want her to come back to me."

Mimi exhales. Flicks the lighter. Inhales. Smoke from two hundred miles away seeps through the phone. "There is no magic that strong, pet. If I could do it, I would."

• • •

After passing the triangle into Key West, the traffic lets up and I cruise down Flagler towards downtown. After scooting around the new City Hall, I park behind the Gato Building, an old cigar factory, and head inside to the BottleCap. The room is dark, decorated in red. A live-results display hangs above the small stage along with television feed from the local television station. At least twenty-five people mill around, but the small room doesn't feel crowded. Red lights illuminate the bar in the corner—I go there first and suck down a double shot of whiskey before asking for a beer. I'm turning to face the stage when I see her.

She wears the emerald shirt I picked out for her all those months ago. The satin shimmers under the lights. The soft fabric shows the outline of her breasts, her bra. Her eyes look like gemstones against the vivid color. "Eli," she says. I stand there, staring. "You're here."

The two shots of whiskey kick in. I clutch my beer. "Congrats," I say.

She gives a soft smile that makes my stomach clench. "We don't know who the winner is yet."

"I have a feeling."

Someone brushes behind her and a faint blush crawls up her neck. She looks down at the floor. "Why are you here?"

In the beginning, before all this, I used to think she was attractive but never beautiful. Now I look at her and she's the most beautiful woman I've ever met. It's in her eyes and her hips and her mouth. The way her expressions soften, then grow hard in fear. "I'm leaving the Keys," I say. "I've got two weeks left."

"Leaving? For what?"

"I'm moving, Carla."

The skin around her eyes crinkles as she squints at me. Her eyes dark back and forth. "Why?"

Deep down, her reaction pleases me. But less so than I thought. It's like a confirmation—the look in her face is enough to let me know this was real, not just some magic that swept over us momentarily. She did care. At least for a little while. "It's just Miami."

"But what happened?"

I stare at her. "What do you think happened?"

She huffs, then turns to look behind her. Jeb talks to people a few feet away but we're buffered by a large group and the loudness of the music. It's dark. Sadness grips me; I hate that the last time I see her will be in a place like this, with the lights down so I can't even get a good look at her. "This is why," she says. "I can't be around this kind of drama."

"Why what?"

She glares.

I clutch my beer. My stomach doesn't hurt like I expected it to. Instead, everything is in my chest. "Can we talk somewhere more private?" Glasses clink behind me. Carla's eyes dart behind me, then to the side of me. There are so many people here. She'll never say yes. I can see it in her eyes now. She's gone steely and cold, somewhere far from me, even though I'm standing right here. "Never mind," I say. "It's your big day."

A country song plays over the speakers. Carla looks up. She's frazzled and I can see it in her cheeks, rosy, despite the cool of the room. I realize she's been drinking, maybe for the majority of the day. "I need to go to my car," she says.

I stand there, stupidly, before realizing she's asking me to go, too. I set my drink on the bar and follow her out, through a crowd of people and into the heat of the night. It's dark out but the streets are full. The smell of cigarette smoke washes over me.

Carla's ass, trapped tight in the black skirt she's wearing, weaves through the people, then out to the Gato Building parking lot. The heat index is still high, though lessened from this summer. It's quieter, here. Just the wave off the palm fronds, the breeze. If I close my eyes and listen hard enough, I can hear the waves.

The collar of her green shirt wavers in the breeze as she walks, not looking at me. "I thought you would stay here forever." But she's not crying. She doesn't look upset at all anymore.

"I can't."

Carla rounds the side of her car. She's backed into the spot and we're at the corner of the lot, shaded under Buttonwoods and next to a chain link fence. I follow, thinking she needs something from the trunk but she stops so quickly I bump into her. She opens the driver's door but doesn't get inside. Instead, she turns her back so she's leaning up against the seat. She looks tan in the soft light, tired. "Are you sure this is a good idea?" she asks.

"Seems like it to me."

"You have such a big business here, though."

"Not anymore."

She squints. "Why?"

I hesitate. Someone walks by but because of the way she's backed into the spot, the trees draped over us and door open, we're invisible. "Jim isn't a fan of me."

Her mouth tightens and then her eyes well up in that unsure, child-like way. "That's not my fault," she says.

"Isn't it?"

She looks at me that way again and it's too much. I reach out and touch her waist, let my hand trail down to her hip. She's full of heat. Her hair, straight today, hangs down in her face. I wish I could be mad at her, but the anger has long since faded. Now, it's just pain. I could cry forever about how much I want her, about how much I wanted things to work out.

I step closer and her breathing quickens. When I lean in, she turns her head so my lips land on the corner of her mouth. She struggles for breath, like her lungs have collapsed inside of her. I bring my hand up to turn her chin, then kiss her mouth. She tastes like orange juice and cigarettes. I step flush against her, so close I can feel the beating of her heart and kiss her harder.

After a moment, she pulls back for air. Simultaneously, her hips buck against me. The look on her face is comical—like she's shocked by her want. Scared. I love that after all these months, I still have the power to make her feel like that.

I kiss her neck, reach down and grab the hem of her skirt. I start inching it upwards and her breathing goes crazy. She grabs my wrists. "Wait," she says. But there's no one in the lot. No light above us. Nothing. I cinch her skirt just high enough on her thighs, then shift so my body covers hers.

She sighs. "Eli—"

"Quiet."

My hand moves around her thighs, feeling the stretch marks, the slight dimples. Her legs widen. Her head tilts back slightly so I can feel her breath on my cheek. She exhales hard. But when my hand moves higher up her thigh, her body tenses. Her head comes forward again. Her leg muscles clench. "I can't," she says. "Stop."

I stop immediately, retracting my hands to look at her. Beads of sweat condense on her chest She puts her hands on my forearms but doesn't push me away like I think she's going to. We stay like that, breathing hard. There's no other sound.

"What, Carla?"

"I can't," she repeats. "I can't deal with the drama anymore."

I shift. We're still pressed against each other, but I'm not moving anymore. A burning feeling stretches across my chest. "This isn't drama. This is me wanting you."

"You don't want me," she says. "You're just playing games."

I try to calm the feeling of need inside me but I can barely stand it. Carla's skin is warm, damp now from sweating. I realize then that this is the best I'll ever get of her—pressed up against her SUV in a parking lot downtown. Slip ups and late nights, like I'm a mistake. I'll never get to bring her on a romantic vacation. There will never be pictures of us. She will never say, "I love you."

I hold her by her wrist, feeling her pulse pound. Part of me can't believe I let this happen, that I let myself fall for her. I can't believe that I'm here again, thirty years old with nothing to my name except a business, being pushed away by someone I really thought might love me.

She breathes hard and her eyes are glossy. I smooth back her hair and wipe the sweat from her upper lip. The streetlamp flickers above us, reflected in her sweat. "Fine." I take a step back from her. "Live drama free, then."

I think maybe I want her to cry. Tell me not to go, or tell me she'll try harder. That we could make things work. But she doesn't. She leans forward off the side of the seat. Fixes her dress. She doesn't look at me. Then she shuts the car door and brushes past me.

THIRTY

Carla walks back inside as quickly as possible and makes her way to the bathroom. Inside, she locks the door and stands with her back against the wall. Her heart races. She stands there, thinking of how stupid she's been over the past year. She tries to laugh.

Eli was just a fling. Just a curiosity. She has to put it behind her.

She takes a deep breath. The air conditioning comes on and the sound of it fills the bathroom. Carla leans forward, off the wall. She goes to the mirror and squints. She looks tipsy. Her eyes are like glass. In the harsh light, the wrinkles around the corners of her mouth are stark. She imagines having to Photoshop them out. Having to paint foundation on. Worrying about close ups in pictures and on the news.

Her chest starts to hurt. She places her hands on the sides of the sink and leans forward. No. Everything will be fine. She won't win tonight. She'll lose by a slim margin and everyone will respect her for the run. She's had a good campaign.

Carla splashes some cold water on a paper towel and starts dabbing at her neck. There are wrinkles there, too. Wrinkles Eli kissed, that she traced at night in bed. Carla blots the lines with the towel. Beads of water condense and roll down her neck, seeping into the neckline of her shirt.

Over the past several months, she's grown her business substantially. Enough to buy a new house, and she might. Miles has a 3.2 GPA at school—better than he's ever done before. Jeb is back in her life, but not all the way. Everything's fine.

The pain in her chest burns like she's dying. Probably heartburn from all the orange juice. Nothing to worry about. She touches the spot, pressing her palm to it. Her pulse throbs. She thinks of Eli, then. Eli at the kitchen counter, palming a beer in bed. She's only bluffing about moving. Playing her little games. And maybe she'll stay mad, but not forever. Eventually they'll be friends again and everything will go back to normal.

Carla stands up straight and smooths out her shirt. Her hands tremble slightly—adrenaline. But it's almost over. Just a few more hours.

She goes to the bathroom door, opens it, and puts on a smile.

THIRTY-ONE

The results come in around five after ten pm. The crowd has thinned by then, but the die-hards are still around. The whole room seems like it's dimmed by fog. Or maybe it's just me. I'm on my third beer, flirting with Monroe County's former representative, Ariana, a woman just younger than Carla who served in Tallahassee.

Ariana is smaller than Carla. Although she has nice hips, I'm not taken by her eyes or smile. Her nose is narrow. She's wearing professional clothes even though she's not the representative anymore, and for some reason this bothers me. What bothers me more is that I'm still here, still waiting for results, flirting with a woman I don't even like just to keep myself from staring at Carla.

I can't leave yet. I have to see the big moment.

"Miami has an amazing art district," Ariana purrs. "You'll love it there."

I sip my drink. "I don't care much for arts," I say. Ariana stares at me. I force my lips into a smile. "Joking. I'll check into it. Thanks."

I turn away from her and hail the bartender. I shouldn't be here; I don't belong. The Keys were never a fit for me. Neither was Carla. Without her, it feels like I'll never belong anywhere.

I'm paying my tab when the screen above the platform goes blank. Then a woman on the screen announces that the results are in from Monroe County.

"Oh, look," Ariana says from behind me. "It's time!"

I turn. The TV screen lights up. I search the audience for Carla and find her standing near Jim and Jeb, looking uncomfortable in her skirt. She fidgets with the hem, her face tilted toward the screen. The light splays across her cheeks. Small and scared.

Jeb ushers her up to the platform. The crowd has grown quiet now.

The newscaster says something then, but I'm not listening. I'm just watching Carla's face. Her eyes widen, and then her face goes white as a sheet. I know immediately. "Oh gosh," says the ex-representative. "I almost can't believe it."

Carla takes the stage. I chance a glance at the television and see that she's won by only a few votes.

Jim says something on the platform. Then Carla smiles out at the crowd. I can't help but think how I love her hair and her eyes and her stupid, unsure smile. Her hips and her voice and the way she is a pain in the ass sometimes but so soft and docile others. I love that she fights for what she wants. I love that she is not afraid to hurt people and I hate her for that, too.

Jim hands her a microphone. There's silence, and then the soft humming of a microphone left silent too long, like electricity coming through the floors. Someone coughs in the corner. Then Carla looks at me. There's nothing triumphant in her eyes. She looks frightened, worn.

I think it will make me feel better about everything, but it doesn't.

A shiver races up my skin. I hold her gaze for a moment. Then I place my beer on the bar top and walk out.

Acknowledgements

Thank you to the Anne McKee Artists Fund for investing in Blindsided. Your support of this project in its very initial stages meant the world to me.

Thank you, Lisa, Kristina, and Andreea for your incredible feedback and support of this piece.

Thank you, Lee Martin, for your edits and encouragement.

Thank you, Vicki, my editor and mentor. Thanks for sticking with me.

Thank you, Daniel R. Ball, my number one reader and best friend. I truly wonder what I would do without you. Your patience in reviewing my writing is a blessing and your friendship, advice, and consistency is something I hope never to take for granted.

And thank you, Bev, for being the Mimi I needed while preparing to leave the Keys.